CARLA'S
SECRET

Carla's Secret

The Wish Granters, Book Two

L B Gschwandtner

ISBN 9780939613595

Cover design by Caroline Murphy
Copy editing and proof reading by Liane DiStefano

MOTHER'S LOVE GROWS BY GIVING.

CHARLES LAMB

Dear Reader:

Let me tell you about two important characters who were introduced in *Book One* of *The Wish Granters* series. Their names are Joe and Alanna. What you need to know about them is this. They're no longer alive. They died in accidents in different places at the very same time. They never knew each other in life but the thing is, they're not technically dead. They're in what's known as "Transition." And they've been sent back to earth as a team to grant one wish at a time to one woman at a time. This time that person is Carla.

If you've ever made a wish and hoped it would come true, this story may reassure you that a wish is never in vain.

One other thing about Alanna and Joe ... they each have unfinished business of their own back on earth.

Chapter One

The high-pitched scream came from somewhere behind Carla's Home Cooking. It lasted only a few seconds, just long enough to catch Carla's attention. She looked up from her account book and pulled her reading glasses down her nose to see over them, as if that could help pinpoint the exact source. It didn't. Not exactly.

At first she tried to shrug it off as just another night sound from the city. Had she really heard a scream? Probably it was a cat fight out back in the alley. Or it could have been a coyote. They'd been spotted in Brooklyn slinking around trash bags after dark.

But something about that scream stuck to her like a burr. She pushed aside the account book she'd been studying and stood up all in one fluid motion, walked swiftly to the back door, unlocked it, and peered down to the right where the short alley behind her restaurant ended in a wall and a series of backyard gardens one after the other, each delineated by its own fence. A construction dumpster to her left partially hid the view in that direction where the alley opened onto the busy commercial street.

Then she heard something else. Scraping and a muffled thump as if something had fallen. The skin on her arms tingled and she knew. She just knew. Past eleven, dark and cold out there now, it was a Thursday night when the alley should have belonged to stray cats and fat rats.

The scream hadn't come from right behind the restaurant because in that case it would have been even louder. Her cook, Raoul—she never referred to him as a chef because that would have caused him to grumble about putting on airs—had gone for

1

the night and Carla was alone. Thoughts whizzed through her mind. If only Raoul hadn't gone for the night. Burly, ex-boxer, Raoul. Nothing on this Earth frightened that man.

Carla's thoughts were eerily clear as she ticked off all the logical possibilities. Lock the door again. Call 911. Grab a sharp knife. Run to the street out front. Flight or fight. Fight or flight. But her phone was in her bag all the way at the front of the restaurant—it might as well have been the other side of the world. It would take the police at least ten minutes to get there after the call, if she was lucky. She'd called them only once before when someone had tried to break in the front door. That time it had taken almost a half-hour for the cops to arrive and, by that time, she'd scared off the would-be burglar on her own.

Carla could manage just about any situation. The block she'd been around could have stretched halfway across the country and she was the kind of woman who could wither with a glance but also melt with a voice of honey. In forty-three years, she'd learned how to make her own way, let nobody get the better of her, but also gather people up like flowers in a bouquet. She was not the kind of a woman who looked away, she told herself, and straightened her spine.

She glanced from the doorway up and down the alley until she spotted a stray two-by-four near the dumpster and ran out into the night, which was never really dark in Brooklyn because cities only feign sleep.

She picked up the solid piece of wood, heavy and just long enough to do the job, and approached the huge dumpster, the detritus of a torn-apart house sticking up from its maw. Quickly rounding the corner of the giant metal box, her stomach clenched and recoiled at the sight of a girl's legs, bare, beige, slender, against the dirty pavement strewn with bits and pieces of drywall and wood and God only knew what else. A faceless man, a white man, large, the muscles of his arms taut with strain, his full body on top of the girl, tearing at something, his shoulders heaving, his unprotected back to Carla.

She approached directly, heart pumping blood hard through her body, energy issuing from somewhere deep down in her core. She held the two-by-four with both hands and raised it as if to cleave a log for firewood and thwack! She came down with it in one sure motion across the man's back, fast, with the force of her weight behind it. Before he could turn completely to face her and, as he fell to one side and she heard the clatter of metal and saw a reflection of light against a blade, she raised the board again and thwack! Without aiming at a specific spot on the man's body, came down across his shoulder and neck.

She didn't feel anything at that moment. Not fear. Not anger. Not even an ounce of hesitation. She was a lioness, protecting a cub that might as well have been her own. The girl lay before her half naked, skirt torn, ripped panties cast aside, long, raw streaks of red that would later turn to a bruised blue on her thighs, a dazed expression on her face, eyes wide as if caught suddenly in the beam of a bright light. It had all happened so fast, she had not yet begun to tremble.

The man moaned. Blood that had started from his neck oozed along his shoulder. His pants were open and Carla tried not to look at what was exposed. She reached down for the girl's hand as gently as she could. It was the better of her impulses because she also had the urge to beat the man until he was nothing but a squashed lump left there to rot in that back alley. The girl took her hand and allowed Carla to pull her up.

"Come on, girl. Come with me away from here."

*

Although their first assignment had resulted in a wish granted, Joe and Alanna were still in Transition. It seemed it would not be easy—or fast—to go back either to the world of the living on Earth, or ascend to the next level, beyond the living. The decision would not be theirs to make in any case, so here they were. They had been called back to stand before Morgan and other members of The Committee. Transition was now a familiar state. They were no longer newcomers to this world beyond life, but not completely accustomed to it either. Transition was an appropriate term. They expected to leave. It was a question of when—and where—they would go.

This time The Committee sat before them not at a long table but in two rows of seats facing a wide, semi-transparent screen that showed the pastel mists behind it.

"Take your seats," Morgan pointed at two empty chairs to one side. He didn't smile.

Joe looked at Alanna as if to say: "What's going on?" This was not like the first time they'd stood before The Committee. They were no longer strangers thrown together by the whims of whoever controlled Transition and beyond. They were veterans as a team now, used to working together.

"I guess we've been called back to get our next assignment," Joe whispered. "So why can't they just let Morgan give it to us?"

Alanna put a finger to her lips. Joe had not settled down at all. Still rambunctious and ready to see how far he could push the system. She stared straight ahead at the big screen with mist rising behind it and wondered if they had been summoned not to receive a new assignment but to be split up and sent in opposite directions. The thought made her nervous and she realized she'd come to depend on Joe. But Morgan was about to speak. That smooth gravelly voice. The soft but immensely commanding presence. It was all familiar.

"Joe," Morgan's voice was stern as he pointed at Joe. "Alanna," he nodded to Alanna. "You've been called back to witness an event that is about to happen in Brooklyn. Please watch."

The screen came alive with what looked like a satellite image panning down from somewhere deep in space. At first all they could see were vague shapes, mottled ridges, greens and blues but soon, as the image whirled and began to settle, they could make out roads and waterways and soon the image floated over a large body of water and moved inland to New York Harbor and across the East River to Brooklyn. It zoomed and then panned down to blocks of streets and then the tops of buildings, right down to an alley between two rows of buildings. Street lights provided some light but it was late and many of the signs on businesses and restaurants had gone dim. The view from up there on the wide screen showed everything at a bit of an angle that made the man they could now see and the buildings near him appear slightly tilted.

The man huddled against a building at the edge of an alley near the sidewalk. They couldn't see his face but they could see he wore only a short-sleeved shirt and his muscled arms were bare. Alanna thought this was strange because it seemed to her it was late winter on Earth although how she knew this was a mystery.

He didn't move. A girl came into view walking slowly on the sidewalk alongside the buildings toward the alley. And it happened so fast that it seemed almost as if the man and the girl simply disappeared. But no. There they were farther down the

5

alley away from the street, the man dragging the girl behind a large dumpster, one hand around her neck.

"What's happening?" Alanna cried. "Why are you showing us this? What's happening to that girl?"

Joe put his hand on Alanna's arm but she pulled it away.

"No. Tell me what's happening." She waved her arms as if she could turn off the screen but the alley and the dumpster were still there although now they couldn't see anything else in this silent movie until a woman came from the back of one of the buildings. They watched as Carla picked up a piece of wood and walked toward the dumpster, the wood held in both her hands at shoulder height. In a few seconds, she came back into view, her arm around the girl, whose clothes were torn, leading her back to the building and they both disappeared inside.

"What about the cops?" Joe asked. "Did they get the cops out there?"

"Why have you shown this to us?" Alanna asked. She gave Joe a withering look.

"That is not the point, Joe," Morgan said.

"Well then what is the point? I mean are we watching TV up here or what?" Joe turned to Alanna and was about to say something else when Morgan raised a small round ball and instantly the screen evaporated and they were all seated in the mist.

"You've been called to receive your next assignment. But The Committee felt it was necessary to show you a bit about her." The Committee members nodded and looked at Joe and Alanna.

"Well I can see why that girl would need a wish," Joe said. "I hope she's all right now. I mean I'm assuming here it was an awful thing she went through."

6

"Indeed it was," said Morgan. "But it's not the girl who you're being assigned."

"The woman?" Alanna asked. "The woman who saved her?"

"Exactly," Morgan nodded again and stood. "You'll be getting new clothes and we've seen to it that you'll have a brief rest before you go back down to grant her wish. Just remember, though, that not all wishes are easy to grant and not everyone knows exactly what they would wish for given the chance."

"Does that mean—" Joe began but a whoosh and a familiar sensation of pressure told Joe and Alanna that they were being transported—The Manifest it was called up here—and they had no idea where they would materialize next.

Chapter Two

They landed at a kind of spa where they each appeared in a thick robe with sandals on their feet. Joe's first thought was about what they had on under their robes, especially Alanna. She looked damned fine in her robe which was a pretty green that set off her auburn hair and graceful neck. Once again, Joe had the feeling that if he ever did make it back to Earth and life, he'd like Alanna to be there with him. Sometimes it was a real shame that they were stuck in Transition like this, not knowing what was going to happen from one moment to the next. Oh well, he thought, might as well make the most of this R and R while it lasted.

A door opened and someone beckoned for him to enter. He'd never seen these people before and they looked a bit odd somehow. What was it about them? As he moved slowly toward the open doorway he realized that none of them seemed to be walking. They were all dressed in flowing gowns—the men and women—and none of them seemed to have feet, or even legs as far as he could tell. But he figured why not, and went through the doorway. On the other side it was warm and pleasant and there was the scent of something in the air. What was it? He couldn't quite remember and that wasn't unusual because much of his memory was still locked away somewhere.

"It's night blooming jasmine." Alanna's voice came to him from somewhere.

"Where are you?"

"I'm not sure. But I recognize that scent. It's common in Florida in the spring and summer but it only blooms at night."

"Does that mean it's night here now?"

But Alanna was gone again and Joe realized he was suspended in a hammock but it was much lighter and softer than a hammock so it was also not a hammock. The not-hammock swayed a bit and he felt comfortable and safe. He closed his eyes but instead of a sweet dream what came to him were bits and pieces of a memory that he'd had before, only this time they made no sense. There was his partner, Russell, and a blonde woman, her head turned away so Joe couldn't see her face. Russell looked angry. That wasn't unusual for Russ. Being law partners, he had learned to accommodate to Russell's moods because he had other, better qualities. Like his ability to make contact with a jury. In a way Russell was everyman to Joe's superman. At least that's what Russ used to call him. Joe had the ability to pull out a save when it was needed most. But in this not-dream, it was clear Russell was in danger and Joe felt helpless to save him.

When Joe opened his eyes, he was no longer in the hammock but seated in an armchair. His sandals had disappeared, a woman was giving him a foot rub, and he realized that the jasmine scent was coming from the oil on his own feet. He heard Alanna laugh but for some reason he couldn't call out to her. If this was R and R, he thought, let's get back to our assignment or at least give us a beer. No sooner had the thought popped into his head than he found himself seated at a long bar and Alanna was laughing at something the bartender had said.

They weren't in robes anymore. Alanna looked great. Like she'd just come from the beauty salon or something and she was wearing a dress he'd not seen before. Around her neck hung a delicate gold chain strung with little blue beads and a small golden amulet in the shape of a triangle. She was certainly a girl you'd want to find sitting next to you at a bar, he was thinking. The bartender slid a tankard toward him and he guzzled it down because he realized he was thirsty and hungry at the same time. While he was emptying the tankard, Alanna moved next to him and signaled to the bartender for another round.

"Remember this drink?" she asked him.

Joe put down the empty mug and smiled at her. "Yeah. I do. This is where we first got to know each other." He took in her face and hair and that long graceful neck with the chain around it. "You look really pretty today. Or is it night? I can never tell up here."

Alanna smiled back. "I know. It's confusing. They gave this to me to wear when we were in that spa place. I guess it doesn't really matter what day or time it is here. It all seems the same. I remember these not-drinks, whatever they are. They still make me feel really good."

It was true. Up there, in Transition, day or night, winter or summer, warm or cold, it was all the same. They finished their second round of not-drinks, knowing that the minute they got comfortable, the minute they settled in for an intimate moment, the minute they started to feel as if their world had some predictability, they'd be pulled away. So without speaking the words, they tacitly agreed on enjoying the moment while it lasted. They raised their tankards and toasted each other and, just as they finished the last drops of their not-drinks, just as Joe reached out to stroke Alanna's arm as a precursor to his next move, the familiar feeling of pressure returned.

Alanna took Joe's hand so they wouldn't be separated on the trip back to Earth but she needn't have clung to him this time for in a single breath they found themselves riding a winged horse through fields of what seemed like lavender flowers but were not flowers exactly and could have been sea fans blowing first this way and then that as if a tide were moving them.

10

"Oh, look, Joe," Alanna pointed to the meadow of not-flowers below them.

Joe held the reins as the great horse soared through the air and Alanna held on around Joe's waist and then boom! They were crashing through space, hurtling down and down. The meadow disappeared and they spiraled in a dizzying swirl of clouds and crystals that stung their cheeks, down and down until they could hear the sounds of a city and they materialized on a busy street in Brooklyn right by the alley that looked all too familiar. The early-morning crowds moved along the sidewalks with purpose. Everyone had somewhere to go, something to do, places where they were expected.

Chapter Three

In the first moments inside Carla's Home Cooking the girl couldn't—or wouldn't—speak.

Carla led her to a table closest to the kitchen and propped the door open giving them a bit of light but not enough to encourage people on the street to think the restaurant was open. She put a teapot on the stove to boil water, took her purse from a small desk set into a corner alcove at the front, and sat down across from the girl.

"I'll have to call the police," she said softly as she rummaged around for her cell phone inside the purse, but the girl didn't look up. "I'll stay right here with you."

She poked in her purse through the amassed accumulation of the bits and pieces of her daily life, likely going back months since Carla never really emptied her purse of nonessentials. Her purse might as well have been an organic part of her body rather than something external she could jettison. The fragments of Carla's life attached to each other as much as they attached to her. When her fingers made contact with the small cell phone she pulled it out and made the call. Then they waited.

The girl sat with her head down. Her torn clothes hung loosely from her body and her dirty fingers clutched the edges of a thin coat that looked too small for her frame. Dried, caked, blood ran along fine scratches on her right wrist. Carla fought the urge to clean her up with a warm cloth, knowing she should wait for the police to arrive so they could see what had happened. Instead she stood up, smoothed her wool skirt over generous hips, and walked slowly to the kitchen to make two mugs of tea, She glanced back at the girl a couple of times just to be sure she didn't bolt but there seemed little chance of that.

12

"Here," Carla set a mug of hot tea down in front of the girl. "What's your name, honey?"

When the girl didn't answer, Carla reached across the table and ever so gently rested the tips of her fingers on the girl's hand and, when the hand was not withdrawn, Carla picked up her own mug of tea.

"They'll be here soon. You've got nothing to be ashamed of."

The girl looked up then and slowly, carefully, pulled her hand away. "Tempest," she said. "My name is Tempest." She dropped both hands to her lap.

There was tapping on the front door glass and, in a moment, the police—a woman in uniform and a detective wearing a suit with a raincoat over it—were inside the restaurant where Carla and the girl laid out the events of earlier that night like a day-old meal. The policewoman wrote notes and looked at her watch now and then. The man, who introduced himself as Detective Lou Mathews, asked personal questions of the girl named Tempest. And soon Carla told her part of the story, trying to keep rage and disgust out of her voice for the sake of the girl. But it was not easy for Carla. She wanted to scream at someone and all that rage shocked and bewildered her.

But she answered the questions. Spoke in a controlled voice. Told the story without embellishment. Yet all the while she felt the urge to scream followed by the need to control tears that threatened to well up at any moment.

When the detective—he was a tall man with chocolate skin darker than Carla's, controlled and professional, with a deep, smooth voice, and eyes that looked as tired as the moon, who had taken off his raincoat by then and laid it across a chair—asked the girl what she was doing out on the street at eleven thirty at night, Carla jumped in for the first time.

13

"Why you ask her a thing like that? Hasn't she got a right to be out whenever she wants? Would you ask a boy that question? Poor thing, after what she's been through."

Carla had an urge to hug the slender white girl to her but something held her back. Maybe it was the way the girl was sitting, the tilt of her chin, or the set of her shoulders. Maybe it was just the situation.

Tempest looked from Carla to Detective Mathews and shook her head.

"I have no place to be really."

"Runaway?" The policewoman asked, her voice as flat as if she'd been through this a million times.

"No," the girl's voice was equally flat. "I'm eighteen. An adult technically so I don't have to answer to anyone. I haven't run away from anywhere. I just haven't found anywhere I want to be."

"Well, you can come right home to my house and stay as long as you like. Tempest. That's a pretty name. I got a room and bath up on the third floor—"

But before Carla could finish the policewoman interrupted with more questions. Did she see the man's face? Could she identify him? Did he say anything? What was his voice like? Did he have an accent? Did he have a weapon? And then the question, asked by the policewoman, had there been penetration? Had he finished?

At that Carla nearly exploded. As if they were asking about a date, about sex between two people rather than about an assault on a teenaged girl. But the girl answered every question in a monotone.

Yes he had been inside her. She didn't know if he had finished and no, she hadn't washed or anything. Yes he had threatened to strangle her if she made a sound. No he didn't

14

have an accent. Yes he was white. And so on and on. And finally, yes she had seen his face. He had a nasty scar above his right eyebrow. It cut his eyebrow in half, she said, and then her eyes closed as if she was trying to recall the detail, or maybe forget the whole thing.

While the policewoman listened to Tempest, Detective Mathews led Carla away from the table and asked her to calm down, telling her that this was all routine, that they had to ask these questions and that she wasn't helping by getting herself all worked up. While he talked to Carla, he studied her carefully.

He liked what he saw, liked the close-cropped hair that said she was not fussy about herself, liked the full, round body that said she enjoyed life, liked the sparkle in her rich, brown eyes and the tilt of her head when she concentrated on something. And he liked the way she defended a girl she didn't even know.

He'd heard about Carla from people in the neighborhood, from the minister who ran the free-meal program at the Baptist church, from other officers on the beat. Carla was well known but Detective Mathews had never actually met her before. He wondered why. Just fate he figured. Or years working vice undercover. You never knew what the next day, or night, was going to bring. Now that he'd moved from vice to crime, he'd been getting around more, meeting more normal people, engaging in life again.

"Well you didn't go out into that alley and see that man on top of her. And you didn't hear her scream. Or see her poor bruised legs or her clothes all tore up," Carla told him and folded her arms across her chest.

"I know this is hard. I see this all the time. I'm used to working sex crimes and I've learned that it doesn't help anyone to add more emotion on top of what the victim has already been through. So just please cool your heels. We still have to get her to the hospital to take samples."

Chapter Four

Carla began every morning with a little ritual. Today, despite the events of the night before, would be no different.

She stood at the back door facing the alley crisscrossed with yellow police tape. She held an oversize stainless-steel bowl Raoul used for mixing biscuit dough. He made biscuits by the double dozen starting at four every morning until the last ones had been sold, usually by ten. In the cool morning the sun peeked down the backyards of the buildings. March was Carla's favorite month although she didn't know quite why. Maybe it was the promise of spring. She liked the warmer air and windy days. There was also a sadness to March, a feeling that something was disappearing but also hope that rebirth was nearby.

"Come on, little ones," she called and made a small chirping sound by pursing her lips together and pulling in. The bowl was filled with scrap food from the day before. "Come on, you little ole fur balls."

She placed the bowl on the concrete block outside the door. The cats came running from behind trash cans, from under the scratched construction dumpster, and from atop a pile of old boards left the month before by a different construction crew. A small black cat with white paws jumped from one of the fences that separated backyards like lined-up dominoes all the way down the alley. Eight cats crowded around the bowl, nudging one another out and moving in from another position until they all finally settled into a mass of hunched shoulders and twitching tails.

Carla stood up, hands on her ample hips. She smiled. "Now ain't that goo-ood?" she said to the cats, slipping into a kind of language she hadn't used in years, words and intonations that came out only when she spoke to the critters, a language from long ago in a southern past she could barely remember, a time that had been nearly wiped off the pages of her memory.

"You be fat and sassy soon." Some of the cats were already fat from eating a steady supply of food every night at closing and every morning when Carla's Home Cooking opened for business.

"Raoul," Carla called turning toward the inside of restaurant, "come look at these kitties."

Raoul came to the door, wiping his hands on a white apron neatly tied around his middle. He was a powerfully built man with muscles that middle age had not softened. Carla met him, a former boxer down on his luck, while he was stirring a vat of stew at a church soup kitchen and she immediately liked his gruff-giant approach. She'd asked him to come cook at her restaurant that very day and he'd been a fixture ever since. Funny thing was, he cooked like a dream. Could make anything. Was always getting new cookbooks out of the library and studying them, then trying out the recipes. He'd placed a chalkboard opposite the counter where patrons would stand and study the day's specials. He'd taken to going out of the city on his days' off to buy fresh produce from the farms. And he frequented the fish market long before the sun rose a couple of mornings a week.

"Humph," he said. "Them cats is overfed, you ask me."

"Who's asking you?" Carla clapped him one on the upper arm. "Wish you'd been around last night. Those muscles coulda come in handy."

18

Raoul frowned. He didn't like for Carla to stay late alone at the restaurant. "What about when you got even more kitties? You just increasin' the problem."

"I already called the lady at the Humane. She's coming tomorrow to take them and get them fixed and find them homes. I told her any of them she got left, she can bring on home to me." Carla squeezed past Raoul. He ran his palm back and forth over his half-bald head. It was his opinion that Carla made herself too vulnerable. Always helping everybody, no matter who they were or where they came from or what they'd done.

"You all right?" he asked in a low voice so as not to worry Carla, but she didn't answer and he figured she hadn't heard him. She wouldn't want him fussing over her anyway, he figured. She was like that. Independent. But she'd told him about last night and about the girl. He would be more watchful from now on, stay later until he saw she got home safely, make sure no one was hanging around in the alley.

He stood there a few more minutes. One of the younger cats came up and rubbed his leg. "Thass a good kitty cat," he mumbled and leaned down and stroked its orange fur. Then he looked up and caught Carla watching him. They both started to laugh.

"You ole thang," Carla crooned. She had heard him and she knew he was worried about her. "You fuss like an old woman."

*

From their position where the alley met the sidewalk, Alanna and Joe watched Carla feed the cats. The way she began each workday had been in her folder. The folder they got with their next assignment. Of all the strange things about Transition, the information folder was one of the most incomprehensible. Just receiving it imparted a wealth of information about Carla and they absorbed it almost by osmosis. Yet the minute they knew everything about her, they knew nothing, only recalling bits and pieces at crucial times when needed. Alanna thought it was like memory. You had no idea how much you had stored up until one day a cascade of it came tumbling out and there it was, right in front of you and you had no idea why.

They saw Raoul come to the back door and watched him stroke one of the cats. Then the door shut and Alanna and Joe looked at the dumpster where the night before a girl had been attacked. There was police tape surrounding the area and then two officers brushed past them, looking very official.

"We'd better get out of here," Joe said and took Alanna by the arm. "Don't want to get mixed up in that." He hugged Alanna close to him and it felt good to walk together like that. If only there was some way to really become a couple, Joe was thinking as he felt the outline of Alanna' hip against him. And then Alanna spoke and Joe realized she was not thinking the same thing so he released some of the pressure on her arm. But not all. He still held her close.

"What do you think happened to that poor girl? She looked so young. And scared."

"I'm sure her parents were called. She looked about fifteen to me. And we don't know if she was actually raped or not, no matter what she said."

Alanna broke away from Joe and stopped right there in the middle of the sidewalk. "How can you say something like that? And you a lawyer. An officer of the court. She was attacked. Whether she was technically raped or not is not the issue. She was violated and frightened and abused. I can't believe you would even—"

"Whoa," Joe held up his hands. "Back off. I didn't mean she wasn't attacked. I just mean we don't know the whole story. After all, we're here for, what's her name? Carla. She's our assignment. Not the girl."

"We can still feel sympathy for the girl. And she said she was eighteen."

"Okay, constable, holster your billy club."

"I think being a lawyer must have turned you into a cynic. A girl doesn't claim to have been raped if she wasn't."

"Being a lawyer made me a realist. And just to set the record straight, women sometimes do claim—"

"Oh just stop it, Joe. I'm not getting into an argument with you about this. Anyway, if you're such a realist, why are you floating in Transition and not back on Earth permanently?"

"That's a non sequitor. One has nothing to do with the other." Joe looked thoughtful, remembering the images of Russell and the woman that had come to him up there in the not-spa.

"You had some more memories didn't you?" Alanna's voice softened.

"How'd you know?"

"I was there too, you know. I think that spa was some kind of memory unlocker. I don't think it was meant for R and R at all. I had some strange visions in there, too. About my fiancé after he walked out."

21

They walked in silence for a few minutes, not heading anywhere particular, crossed a street at a traffic light and halfway down the next block found themselves in front of Carla's Home Cooking.

Alanna was admiring the display of blooming orchids in the front widow when Joe said, "Look" and pointed as he peered in the window. "It's open. Let's go in for breakfast. Might as well meet our next assignment."

Chapter Five

Sometimes it seemed as if Carla was feeding half of Brooklyn. She seemed to attract people the way light attracts moths. Well people are not much different from the stray cats, she thought. Offer them food and safety and they're drawn in. There were her regulars. Marv, for one.

Carla had seen him confronting a large, aggressive-looking Norway rat in the alley behind the restaurant. She spotted Marv's rumpled old felt hat first and then noticed how gaunt and shaky he was so she invited him to come in and have some stew. She was always careful about that. No matter how downtrodden, she treated everyone all with respect. That was two winters ago when it had turned bitter cold and Marv left the subway tunnel where he slept only when the weather allowed him to scrounge.

After that first meal, he came in for stew a couple of times a week, never asking for anything else but always bringing something for Carla. A newspaper, a wire hanger, a desk lamp with a burned-out bulb, and sometimes an orchid plant. Rich people on Manhattan's upper east side regularly threw them away, especially after holidays. On trash days he traveled by subway on nickels and dimes he found—or begged for—on the sidewalks, got off at Bloomingdales, and walked the cross streets between Lexington and Fifth Avenues collecting the castoffs of the rich.

Carla placed all the orchids in the front window of her restaurant. Under her care, they came back to life. Besides the array of enticing blooms, in the early morning Carla's Home Cooking was filled with the sweet scent of freshly baked muffins. This was what greeted Alanna and Joe when they walked through the door and were seated at a booth by the front window by a young woman who placed breakfast menus in front of them.

"You folks here for the flapjacks? Best in Brooklyn, you know. Rated by those people from Zagats."

It was Carla, standing next to their booth, a big, welcoming smile on her face, hands on her hips. She wore a green dress with a big flower print, and pinned to her right shoulder was an orchid in a silver pin that held a tiny bit of water to keep it fresh.

Alanna smiled up at her. "That's a beautiful orchid. What kind is it, do you know?"

"This one's a cattleya. Has a sweet almost-lemony fragrance."

She leaned down for Alanna to take a whiff.

"Oh yes," Alanna said and smiled, "it does. That's really nice. I see you have more orchids in the window."

"All gifts from a friend. He brings them in sick and I nurse them back to health at my house and then bring them on over here. Makes a pretty display in that window. I didn't know anything about them and when they started showing up like that, well I just had to go and learn. So now I know who's who and what to do to make them happy."

Carla kept up a bubbling chatter because she was one of those people who talk and watch at the same time. She read people by osmosis, by how they held themselves and how they moved, by the lilt of a voice, the tilt of a chin, the depth of color in the eyes, by the spaces between words and by the words they chose when they did speak. She had learned that people don't say what they really mean or mean what they say and that you had to come up with sound assessments of character by other means. She sized up Alanna and Joe as tentative and cautious.

24

Why, she was not sure. Maybe they were really with the police. After last night, Carla's guard was up and she carefully avoided any talk beyond pleasantries. Anyway, these two were customers so she asked what they'd like to have and, without writing down anything she turned and headed for the kitchen.

"So how are we going to get her to tell us her wish?" Joe asked as soon as Carla had left.

"Can't we eat first? Alanna scowled at him. "For the first time since we entered Transition, I'm actually hungry."

"Anything you want, my sweet. I live to make you happy."

"Right. Except you're not exactly alive."

"A technicality that I plan to remedy soon."

"And how do you plan to do that?"

"I have a feeling I'm going to solve all those memory fragments I've had about Russell and an elusive woman and a guy with a gun."

"Sounds scary." Alanna meant to say more but their food arrived on a big round tray that, because the waiter held it in a precarious balancing act between his left hand and left shoulder, hid his face from them. He turned away to set it down neatly on a tray stand and came back with individual plates to serve their food—hotcakes, coffee, juice, maple syrup, mixed berries, and small muffins in a basket with an assortment of jams in little pots. Clearly, Carla meant for her restaurant to be more than a hash-and-dash joint.

"But what have you remembered exactly?" Alanna reached for her fork and knife, positioning them above the stack of pancakes that looked so light they might float up to meet her.

A low, mellow, and altogether familiar voice said, "Enjoy that, now."

They both looked up to see Morgan in black pants and a white shirt, a half apron around his waist and an order pad stuck in the pocket. He was grinning. Morgan often appeared to them with a big grin on his face, as if he found the whole idea of Wish Granters intensely amusing.

"What are you doing here?"

"You need my help, don't you?"

"We just got here. We're still figuring out what's happening. Maybe we'll need your help later but now we're just fine. And Alanna wants to down those pancakes. So maybe we can have a few minutes off?"

"That true? You want pancakes more than you want to grant this wish so you can get out of Transition?"

Alanna glanced from her pancakes, to Joe to Morgan and then back at her plate. She wondered where Carla had gotten to and what the others working in her restaurant thought about Morgan appearing suddenly to wait tables.

"How do you get away with this stuff?" she asked him. "We've seen you as a bartender, a cab driver, and now you're a waiter. Doesn't anyone ever get suspicious when you just show up?"

Morgan chuckled and nodded at Alanna's plate. "You better eat up while it's hot. You're about to have a busy week, I believe." He turned to Joe. "Cab driver is my favorite alternate occupation. And did it ever occur to you two that no one else can see me the way you do?"

With that he turned, picked up his round tray and walked toward the kitchen.

"I don't know what he means about needing help. We haven't run into any trouble yet." Joe picked up his fork.

"Except for the little problem of how to get Carla to tell us her wish," Alanna said softly as she put a forkful of warm pancake smothered with warm, sweet maple syrup into her mouth.

26

Chapter Six

They decided Alanna would leave her wallet behind so she would have an excuse to come back later to retrieve it. They figured since Carla had been there the night before, she probably stayed late every night to close up and tend the account books. Only problem was, since they'd ascended to Transition, they'd never had any money or credit cards or any earthly possessions except the clothes they wore, which seemed to change without them asking for new ones, like the coat and scarf Alanna had on when they'd landed in Brooklyn. It had been confusing at first but they'd given up trying to understand how things worked and simply accepted that whatever they might need to accomplish their task would be there when they needed it. So it didn't surprise them that, when the check for breakfast came, Alanna discovered a lovely red-leather purse on the seat by her leg. And Joe reached into his jacket pocket to find a slim leather wallet full of cash containing two tickets to a Knicks game.

"Wow," he held them up to show Alanna. "I think we're going on a date." He smiled at her. "Our very first one. What do you suppose it means?"

"Maybe they're not for us." Alanna felt a small twinge somewhere below her hips. A familiar feeling but one she hadn't felt for a long time. And a memory slipped by as if she had slipped into a dream. The man who had walked out of her life as he opened the door with a briefcase in his hand and a scowl on his face. She looked up to see Joe watching her.

"Still hung up on him, huh?"

Alanna tilted her head to one side and breathed deeply. She wished it were as simple as just letting go of the past. Just walking away or rather letting the past walk away. Yet here they were, she and Joe, caught in Transition, each with a past to sort out, each wanting to move ahead, being attracted to each other and unable to do anything about it.

She had finished eating and laid her knife and fork down. They had paid the bill. Slowly she reached her hand across the table and touched the tips of her fingers to Joe's. He responded as she knew he would. Quickly, with authority and determination. Joe was that kind of a guy. He took her hand in his and raised it to his lips and as he was about to press his lips to her fingers, a chilly wind swept past them.

"Maybe these tickets aren't real," he mumbled. "But we can still have that date."

*

There was something vaguely familiar about the girl yet Joe couldn't quite figure out what it was. Alanna said they should leave but Joe lingered at the table, glancing furtively at the teen who entered Carla's and went to a small table for two near the kitchen. She was dressed oddly, he thought. But didn't quite know what was off about her.

"Do you notice something not quite right about her?" Joe asked Alanna and nodded toward the girl.

"Well her clothes are all way too big for her. And her face is bruised and so is her hand, it looks like. She must be the one who was attacked."

At that moment the door opened and a tall, husky, dark-skinned man wearing a raincoat over his suit walked in. The girl looked up dreamily, as if she was half asleep, and studied the

28

man. The next moment, Carla emerged from the kitchen and waved the man over to the table where she pulled up a third chair and sat down next to the girl. They were too far away for Joe and Alanna to hear what they were saying.

"This would be a great time to be invisible," Alanna whispered to Joe.

"Then let's go outside and find a place where we can transform."

"Where could we do that in a busy place like this?"

"How about that back alley?"

"Perfect. Let me just tuck my wallet down here where no one else will find it."

She slid the wallet to the very end of the booth where the back met the seat, wedging it in tight so it was hidden from view. It was an odd feeling not to care about the money in her own wallet. But after all, it wasn't her money and she didn't really have any possessions anymore. That was a liberating feeling, she'd discovered. Not to have to care about things. If she ever did go back to life, she wondered how her time in Transition would have changed her. Maybe she would never want to be burdened by possessions again. On the other hand, how could anyone live without them? At least on Earth. If she went on to her next dimension, she wondered if there would be any possessions. Maybe whatever you needed would appear as you needed it. That would be pleasant, she thought, but then a nagging feeling took hold and she realized that having everything you needed handed to you might not be such a good thing. In any case, no one could hand you the solutions to your life's puzzle. She was sure of that. Here she was in Transition and still wondering about the problems from the life she used to have. Like Joe, she had an unrelenting urge to settle her unresolved business.

Joe stepped carefully around the perimeter of the crisscrossed yellow police tape, looking intently at the ground. It was a mess back here, he thought. A really awful place to be attacked. Of course it had been dark then and you wouldn't have been able to see everything he could see now. Still, it might have been even more scary at night. Especially for a teenaged girl, alone, being dragged back here. He shivered at the thought and it occurred to him that one of the reasons he'd become a defense attorney was to support victims of the system. It hadn't turned out exactly like that. There had been a few cases of wrongly accused clients but for the most part, the money was in getting the guilty the best deal possible. In some cases getting them off entirely. That was rare as well but still not what he'd expected in the beginning. Russell, though, he knew the score from the start.

"This is creepy," Alanna said. "Let's get this done and get out of here."

"How exactly do you do the disappearing? I only did it that one time back in Vegas for the poker game. But I can't remember exactly how it went."

"I think we just sort of relax and think about needing to be invisible and it happens." Alanna shrugged.

As they stood there, Joe had the strongest urge to put his arms around her, even in this place, surrounded by debris and filth. When he looked at Alanna, he forgot where he was and what he was supposed to be doing. So he reached out and touched the side of her face, stroked her hair, and moved close to her.

"Joe," she said softly.

"Yes?"

"We're not supposed to . . ."

"I know. But remember when we were in that chapel in Vegas? We were just starting to . . ."

But his voice began to fade and as he touched Alanna's shoulder in a caress, she began to disappear and he realized that in a few seconds they would be invisible and unable to act on any earthly impulse. Before he could say another word they were back inside the restaurant watching and listening. The man had taken off his raincoat and slung it over a chair. The girl and Carla were seated at the back table. The man pulled out a chair and sat down opposite them.

Chapter Seven

"Now could you identify this man again? Maybe if you looked at a photo array down at the station?"

"She's not ready for any of that kind of business yet," Carla spoke for Tempest.

"Yes, ma'am, I know that but I need to hear from the victim about the crime. We have the test results but that's not enough. Bodily fluids will only take an investigation so far. We need the victim's statement and an identification if at all possible. Of course there is the blood on that piece of wood you used. How did he manage to get up and leave after you struck him?" This time he looked straight at Carla and smiled.

He had even white teeth and when he smiled his face softened and Carla thought he was really quite a handsome man. Big powerful shoulders, salt and pepper hair, and his voice, something about it was reassuring. He held himself well, she thought. Like he was very confident. She liked that. And it surprised her that she liked it.

"I have no idea. I was concerned about this girl here and not about that piece of filth."

"Yes, ma'am. I understand. But you must have gotten a look at him."

"Not any part of him that could help you identify him."

"Are you sure? Did he turn around at any time?"

Carla thought about that for a moment. He had turned. After the first time she struck him. He had turned to his side and she had seen . . .

"Yes," she said slowly. "When he turned and looked up at me. He was large. And white. His arms were bare and I thought

32

that was funny since it was cold outside. His pants were undone. I didn't know how much he'd done . . ."

Carla's voice trailed off and a faraway look appeared on her face as if she had been transported. And then her mouth clamped shut and she sat up very straight, her back stiff and her shoulders squared.

"That's all I remember."

"Would you be able to identify him?"

"No."

"Would you be willing to try?"

"I've got nothing else to say."

Detective Mathews leaned back, tilting his chair on two legs. This was odd, he thought. Usually witnesses wanted to remember every detail of a crime. In fact he'd found there were often too many details and too much information, usually half of it imagined or embellished. This was odd indeed. This woman was a mystery to him. He'd have thought she'd want to remember everything so they could nab this guy. There had been a series of attacks on women in the area. Detective Mathews had pieces of descriptions. He wanted to solve this one. It was his neighborhood, too. He lived not ten blocks away.

"Well," he began. "I don't want to worry you but this is not the first episode we've had and the more information we can gather, the more likely we'll be able to catch this predator and get him off the street. You'd like that, wouldn't you, miss?" He addressed this to Tempest but she just shrugged. This didn't surprise him since she was only a teen and especially the ones who'd taken to the streets were hard to reach. He doubted that this was her first run-in with something bad. But he couldn't drag anything out of her.

"Anyway, we do have that blood. So that should help us a lot. I'll leave you my card. Call me if you have anything else at all. And I'll be around the neighborhood watching things. I have another local case I'm working, so if you need me, my number's on the card. Call any time at all." He smiled at Carla again.

She had relaxed somewhat and this time she smiled back.

"Before you go, how about some coffee and a muffin? We usually run out by this time but I'm sure I could find one or two still warm in the kitchen."

*

"That didn't tell us much, did it?" Alanna turned to Joe after they'd watched the whole exchange.

"Maybe we're missing something here." Joe moved over to one of the windows full of blooming orchids. "What could this woman want that she doesn't already have?"

"She obviously has money, so that can't be it."

"Yeah, she's successful all right."

"And people love her. This place is always packed, it seems."

Joe looked around the restaurant. Alanna was right, the place was packed and it was even an odd time of day. Between early breakfast and business lunch. What he saw were mommies and preschool-age kids, what looked like college kids who probably were between classes, and an assortment of others not so easy to identify. These were like the people who hung out at Starbucks with their laptops open and phones in their hands, nursing lattes, just being in the moment. Except this wasn't a chain; this was a local woman who'd created a niche for herself.

"Maybe that's the answer," Alanna mused.

"What is?"

"That she has everything. Except one thing. Where's her lover or husband? Where's her family? Maybe she's collecting all this love because she doesn't have any in her life."

"Why do women always go right to the relationship equation? Huh? Maybe she's organized her life just the way she wants it."

Alanna glared at Joe. "You can be so annoying. What is that, some kind of bait?"

Joe grinned and, if they both hadn't been invisible, he would have given her a little fist bump on the arm.

"Oh, I see," Alanna nodded, "it was a bait. You're a rogue."

"And you're an easy mark, beautiful. You always jump right at it."

"In any case, I doubt that she's got everything she wants in her life. I mean, maybe she really wishes she had a family. Maybe that's what Morgan wants us to find out."

"Only one way to know for sure. When you go back to get your wallet after she closes for the night, get her talking girl talk and let it just sort of leak out of her. People can't keep their secret wishes and regrets to themselves."

"You think Carla has a secret regret?"

"Has to be or we wouldn't be here. That's one thing. And then there's that girl. There's something familiar about her, but I can't figure out what. Does she seem odd to you?"

Alanna stared at the girl named Tempest and for the first time really studied her. She was thin, almost too thin. Her long hair was straight and black. Completely black without a hint of reddish tint. She was pretty, with white skin so pale it looked as if she hadn't been outside in years. She had big, sad, brown eyes and her oval face was unusually perfect in its symmetry. Especially sitting next to Carla, whose skin was a rich mocha brown, Tempest looked as if she'd been wrung out. Of course,

Alanna thought, the girl had been attacked and she was still upset. She'd been poked and prodded and now here was Detective Mathews grilling her again. Anyone would seem frail and faded after all that. But Joe was right. There was a transparent quality about her in a china-doll sort of way and, yes, something familiar, too.

"One thing though," said Joe.

"What's that?"

"She's a looker."

Chapter Eight

It didn't take long for Carla to incorporate the girl, Tempest, into her life.

It was Carla who accompanied the policewoman and Tempest to the hospital to let the technician collect samples. It was Carla who comforted Tempest throughout the clinical process. It was Carla who supervised the interview with the police, and it was Carla who took Tempest into her home and helped her wash and change her clothes and finally fall into a fitful sleep that first night. The next morning it was Carla who rummaged around in an old clothes bin to find Tempest something—anything—to wear so she could give the police what she'd been wearing the night of "the incident," as Carla referred to it. And it was Carla who accepted that Tempest had no one to contact after the crime—no family or friends or place to go. So it was Carla who offered Tempest a small room on the third floor of her house just a few blocks from Carla's Home Cooking. But it was Tempest who went along for the ride without saying a word.

Tempest's was not the only occupied room in Carla's house.

Marv had moved in a few months after he and Carla had met, over the vociferous objections of Raoul, who considered it his personal mission to protect Carla from harm.

One afternoon, after Marv had cleaned up, gained weight, and gotten back on his feet, there came a soft tapping at Carla's front door. When she opened it, Marv was standing there with a wriggly little mutt named Bugs by his side. Bugs liked Carla right away. His tail wagging furiously, he cocked his head to one side expectantly, probably responding to the scent of stew coming from the kitchen. Carla always had something on the stove or in the oven.

"No, Bugs," Marv told him. "No food for you. He followed me and I couldn't turn him away," he explained to Carla. "You know how that is."

"Indeed I do, sugar." Carla noticed that Marv was holding a small gift-wrapped box.

"You all come on in," she motioned them inside, leaning over to pat Bugs on the head. His tail beat happily against the door jamb, thump, thump, thump.

"I wanted to give you something for being so very kind to me. I wanted to thank you for helping me get back on my feet." He handed her the box.

Carla took it, surprised by his sudden offering.

"Aw, go on with you," Carla said, smiling. "I didn't do nothing but help out a soul who was down on his luck. You did the rest all your own self. Now what's in here?" She rattled the box a little. "You come in and set."

They went to her living room, which was one of the loveliest rooms in the old house although it had seen better days. She had purchased the house from an estate. It was furnished and she'd kept most of the former owner's things. It was of an old European style, formal, plush, dark, lots of wood trim and big windows. Ancient oriental rugs on the floor and dim, crackled paintings on the walls. Carla had added a bit of her own personality, however, and there were plants everywhere, growing in profusion, large, spreading, flowering, climbing, as if the inside of the apartment wanted to be an outdoor garden. Generous light came from the windows almost as high as the enormously tall ceilings, which gave the room an air of grandeur coupled with a formality from an era long gone.

Carla unwrapped the gift slowly, saying it should really go under a tree, that Christmas was past until next year, and presents should wait until next year. But she was obviously happy the way a child would be at the thought of getting a look at one of the presents ahead of Christmas. She lifted the gift out of the box. It was a small silver clock with tiny carved flowers around its face and little vines for feet.

"Oh, my," she said. "This is the most beautiful thing I ever saw. Thank you, Marv. You're a good soul, truly."

Marv grinned at the success of his gift.

Marv felt he owed Carla much more than this little gift. He saw how she fed and nurtured the stray cats. And heard other people talking about her on the street coming and going from the restaurant. The talk was always about how Carla had helped this one or that one, how Carla Patterson was such a good soul, how Carla Patterson was the neighborhood's best friend. So he found the clock in a thrift store by the church. He polished it and took it apart and figured out how to make it work like new. They set the time and she placed the little clock on the mantel.

"This pretty clock on the mantle like that, it really needs a good old-fashioned crackling fire. But this old chimney won't draw. so I guess we'll have no fire here next winter either."

That's when Marv knew just how to repay all the good Carla had done.

"I could get that fireplace working for you, if you like," Marv offered. "And I could bring up some wood. It might be nice to have a fire going on cold nights when you come back from the restaurant."

"Yes," Carla said. "That would be nice. I'd appreciate that."

"Carla?" Marv began.

"What's on your mind?"

"I wanted to tell you something about myself."

39

"About what happened to you?"

"Yes," he said.

"It's always good to unburden yourself."

"You probably wondered how I sank so low."

"I figured you had trouble is all. You know we're all connected in some way," Carla said. "And when one of us starts to fall, we've all got to get together and lift him back up. No other way to survive in this world."

"Not everyone feels the way you do," said Marv. "Most people, when they see someone down like I was, they act as if he's invisible. He no longer has any value to other people and he becomes like a rat in a crevice, hiding and watching for a chance to dart out and take something he needs. People feel threatened by that. And they want to eradicate it like they would that rat."

So Marv told of how he'd been an architect, with a wife and hopes of starting a family. Then the economy went sour, interest rates shot up, people stopped building, and he was fired in a downsizing that knocked out almost half his company's employees. From that day, Marv's world began to fall apart. Everything he had worked for slipped away like a mist. He couldn't get another job because all the firms had been hit. He began to stay out late because he was too ashamed to come home and face his wife. He started drinking, going from bar to bar until one day he came home to find his wife had packed up and left. She filed for divorce. He couldn't pay the rent and was evicted. He sold his car for cash to stay afloat for a short time, but then he went through everything he had until one day he found himself with nothing at all. He ended up in a homeless shelter and then on the street. So he began to wander, scrounging what he could, begging sometimes, stopping at church suppers when he heard of them, going from one dumpster to the next, finally ending up in the alley behind Carla's cafe.

"And now, because of you, I have a life again. I may not be ready to start all over or go back to where I was, but at least I'm not a train wreck anymore," he concluded.

So Marv accepted Carla's offer and moved into her house. Because he couldn't pay any rent, he fixed the fireplace and then remodeled the downstairs bathroom and then the upstairs bathrooms, and then he recaulked the windows and insulated the attic and refinished the wood floors. He went from room to room, refurbishing, rewiring, renovating. Bugs followed along and, after a time, Carla found her house transformed from outdated to stylishly current. When neighbors saw what Marv had done they asked if he could help them, and soon he was bringing in money again and paying rent and making his own way. Yet he stayed on at Carla's, as long as she would have him, he said.

And when Tempest arrived, Marv welcomed her. But for some reason Bugs skulked out of the kitchen the very first morning she came in for breakfast and never would go near her after that.

Chapter Nine

Alanna made sure to materialize outside Carla's Home Cooking just before closing time. Joe waited in a beer bar at the corner. There were still a few people sitting on stools staring at a football game on the flat screen above the hanging racks of glasses. When Alanna evaporated out of the bar, Joe had been placing a bet against another patron's favorite team. He was laughing and hardly noticed she'd left. Joe, she thought, could get along anywhere, any time, with anyone.

It was Tuesday, a slow night for dining out, and the restaurant was empty except for Carla, who sat at a back table with a stack of receipts and a calculator. Alanna peered through the front door-glass and saw Raoul come out of the kitchen wiping his hands on a white apron stained with the remnants of whatever he'd cooked that evening. His skin was walnut brown, his hair cropped so close it was almost invisible. He moved with the grace of an athlete yet there was something vulnerable about him, Alanna thought as he came into full view. Or no, maybe it wasn't what she thought at first. Maybe it was a protective air about him, as if he was Carla's big brother. Alanna wished she could hear what they were saying to each other.

Funny, she thought, we can grant wishes for others but not for ourselves. For a moment her mind wandered from the task at hand to what she would wish for if she could. She sighed and hunched her shoulders against a cold gust of wind. She'd want to see him again—her fiancé. One last time. To see him and tell him exactly why they would never have worked out. But it was too late now. He would have long ago given up on any hope of finding her alive. But if she could meet him just once more. If only . . .

She pushed the door open. A mixed aroma of soups and desserts and baked breads lingered in the warm air. Carla glanced over her reading glasses halfway down her nose. She seemed surprised, Alanna thought, to see anyone in the restaurant at this time of night.

She was right. Carla was surprised, and a little wary after what had happened. But Alanna looked familiar. Carla couldn't possibly remember all her customers but she stood up anyway and then did recall that this one had talked about the orchids in the window. She'd been with a young man.

"I'm sorry to come in so late. I guess you're closing. But I lost my wallet somewhere today and I thought maybe I left it here." Alanna smiled, trying to strike a friendly pose.

It was a plausible story but Alanna was not in the least concerned with that wallet. Since she'd been in Transition, whenever she'd needed money or anything it simply appeared. It was Morgan, of course. He could make anything happen. Or not happen. So instead of being concerned about the wallet, she wondered how she was going to get this woman to talk to her, to share a confidence with her, to open up about anything really, much less to share something as personal as a wish. With the other one it had been easy. At least for Joe. But this time he'd handed the baton to her so she had to run with it.

"You were sitting over here, weren't you, honey?" Carla walked to the booth where Alanna and Joe had been that evening and Alanna followed her.

What if this goes too fast she was thinking? If I find the wallet I'll have no reason to engage her in conversation.

"Which side did you sit at, sweetie?" Carla asked. She looked carefully at the floor but there was nothing under the table.

"I hope I find it," Alanna stalled. "I've never lost my wallet before. Have you ever lost anything?" Alanna said it casually, without thinking much about what made her ask, but Carla suddenly sank down on the edge of the booth seat, with her feet sticking straight out and her hands clasped in her lap. Her friendly smile had vanished. She sighed deeply and tilted her head to one side as if she was listening for some subtle noise, some small voice that would speak the words she herself was struggling not to utter.

"I guess I lost just about the most precious thing anyone can lose in this life," Carla almost whispered, which seemed incongruous to Alanna, Carla seeming like such an exuberant person.

Alanna sat down opposite her and leaned her elbows on the table. She didn't say anything. It seemed right to stay silent. As if she was some sort of therapist waiting for Carla's heart to open to her. Carla's Home Cooking had become a confessional, with Alanna the confessor and Carla's the heart that needed to unburden its secrets.

Carla raised her head slowly, and there was the hint of tears in her eyes. She stared at Alanna but it was not Alanna she was seeing. Still Alanna waited. Carla's lips parted slightly, she licked them and rubbed her hand against her chin and then felt her stomach. She swung her legs around so her feet were under the table now and she was facing Alanna.

"You know what happened here last night?" she asked, and Alanna nodded yes, all the while gazing into Carla's eyes, seeing the pain there, and something else. What was it?

44

"You heard about it. Mmm-hmm. Everybody heard about it. All up and down this street and all over the neighborhood. Everybody's on watch now. I guess that's about the worst thing can happen to a young girl. Even though she's not so young. Says she's eighteen. I don't believe it but that's what she says. She's at my house now, resting. Been through a lot last night and again today. Poor thing." Carla stopped talking and then repeated it. "Poor thing."

"It must have been awful, frightening and brutal. It will take her a long time to heal."

Carla looked past Alanna without answering. She's not hearing me, Alanna thought. She's not here, not completely thinking about the girl, but about something else.

"Barely twelve," Carla said it so softly Alanna was not sure what she'd heard. "Just a young girl not yet grown enough to know what was happening to her." Alanna realized Carla was talking about some other girl.

"Came on her like a branch broke off a tree in a storm. Just like that." Carla snapped her fingers, then let her hand drop in a fist onto the table where it stayed as she continued telling her story, words bubbling over like a stewpot on a hot stove. And the story poured out of someone blindfolding her, of men binding her arms behind her with rope, dragging her through underbrush, sticks cutting at her legs, tearing her cotton dress. Of how the girl was on her way home from school, had stopped to take a book out of the library, a book of poetry, for she was a serious girl who loved the sound of language. Of how she wanted to scream, to bite, to run, but the arms holding her were powerful and she quickly became a voiceless victim. It happened fast she later realized, but at the time it seemed to go on forever like the night sky turning darker and darker still. She tried not to hear the men, not to inhale their odor, turned her face to the side to breathe in the rich earth and desiccated leaves, wished a fox would come and attack, wished for anything to save her.

"Why am I telling you all this? A stranger." Carla looked at Alanna as if seeing her there for the first time. "Maybe it's like going to one of those priests in a booth. Maybe a stranger's the only person you can tell the whole story to. If you tell those that love you, it gives them your pain and then you've got that burden on your soul, too."

Alanna reached out and briefly laid her hand on top of Carla's fist. She let her hand rest there for a few seconds, until Carla released the fist. "It happened to you, didn't it? When you were a girl."

Alanna was aware in a vague way that Raoul had come out from the kitchen to stand behind the bar. He was too far away to hear Carla's story but he watched silently, standing with his arms folded across his chest in case he was needed. Maybe he knew the story already and that's why he was so protective of Carla. Or maybe he didn't know it but felt there was something about her that needed protecting. Whatever it was, Alanna knew that Raoul would be all over anyone who tried to interfere with Carla or threaten her. But Carla was either unaware of his presence or so used to it that she accepted his hovering as normal.

"I think that's why what happened here last night took me so personal, if you understand."

Alanna nodded and gently said, "I can understand that. And more."

It was a rule that wish granters couldn't tell who they were until the woman they'd been assigned made her wish. This was one of those times when it was terribly difficult for Alanna to keep silent about her mission, and she wondered briefly what would happen if she spilled the secret now before the wish had been spoken. Would Morgan suddenly swoop down and haul her back up there—wherever "there" was? She might be punished, or worse, her choices about what happened to her next might be revoked.

Carla lowered her voice so Raoul couldn't hear. "My people were country folk down in Georgia. Where we lived everybody knew everybody. Black and white. Times were different then for black folks. We had to be careful. It wasn't nothin' like it is up here in Brooklyn. I was just a girl but I remember like I was still there today. We had a farm. A big garden and animals. Mama and Daddy grew or raised all our food. Chickens and pigs and cows for milk. Goats and rabbits. And vegetables? Lord, those were the best ripe, garden-fresh foods. I was happy. Until that day that just about changed everything for me." Carla stopped talking for a moment and looked from the window, back to where Raoul stood still as wood, then back to Alanna.

"I'm sorry, honey. I guess I about talked your ear off. And here you just came in to find your wallet. Is it here where you were sitting with that young man?"

Alanna knew it was there but she didn't want this to be the end of it. She had her assignment and she might never get another chance to be alone—or almost alone—with Carla, but she didn't see any way to avoid finding that wallet, so she reached her hand down to where she'd stashed it and pulled it up. "Here it is," she said with a tinge of regret in her voice. And then, for she had nothing to lose but an opportunity, and maybe there was more to it than what she'd heard so far, she asked Carla to tell her the rest of the story.

Chapter Ten

" I beat Boots here with this dollar. I bet on six sevens. Couldn't beat that." Joe nodded to a middle-aged man looking particularly glum seated next to him at the end of the bar.

Alanna took in the empty glasses lined up in front of Boots and reached for the dollar Joe held up to the dim light. "I think you've both had enough for tonight."

"Yeah that's what my wife is gonna say. I gotta go home now and she's gonna go through my pockets. She always goes through them when I come home. Drunk or sober, now that I think of it, but worse when I'm drunk."

He sighed again and slid off the barstool. "You beat me fair and square Joey. You're a regular guy." He stumbled off towards the door and Joe turned to Alanna with a big grin on his face.

"So I made us five bucks, what did you do? Did you get the wish?"

"Boots? I leave you alone for an hour and you take up with someone named Boots?"

"Between you and me, I don't think that's his real name. I think maybe he kicks the"—Joe caught himself before he said it— "stuff out of people for a living. He didn't seem like the most highly advanced specimen on the Darwinian chart. So, what about it? Find the wallet? Get the wish?"

"Oh, Joe. It's not what I ever would have expected. I mean, women wish for beauty, or health for their children, or romance. But Carla . . . well, all I can tell you is she's an amazing woman."

"World peace? Is that what she wants? Because I think that's a little out of our league. Anyway, good for you that you got her to talk."

"It was more than that, Joe. She poured her heart out to me. Told me things she's told only one other living soul. And he was standing by the kitchen door the whole time I was there. Like some spirit guide. It was kind of creepy and kind of comforting at the same time. I don't know how to describe it really."

Alanna told the story to Joe, just the way Carla had told it to her. She told about the attack, about how the men had tied Carla's arms and blindfolded and gagged her. Once Alanna got into the story, Joe stopped teasing and kidding around. He took hold of her arm and held it tightly as she related the story in a hushed voice.

The men never said a word, Carla had told her. She never saw any detail of what they were wearing or anything else about them, except she could smell the liquor on them. Even at twelve, she knew that smell. It could have been anyone, but she knew somehow, knew they were white boys, and she had a feeling just which ones they were.

After it was all done they left her there in the woods alone. She didn't know how long she lay there on the forest ground but finally she was able to roll over and get to her knees. She was frightened. Maybe one of them was still there. Maybe he wouldn't let her get away. She tried to walk but stumbled. She didn't know which way to go, and then she tripped over a fallen tree trunk and her arms struck a branch that had split into a pointed spike of wood. It hurt, but she also realized she could use it to loosen the rope and she rubbed against it carefully until she felt it grab the rope, and she pulled and tugged until she felt it loosen. Well, that was her first step. She untied the blindfold and found her way home. When her mother saw her come into the yard, she screamed and rushed to Carla.

Carla's parents were older when they had her. A religious couple who spent every Sunday in church and never said a bad word about others, they kept to themselves and worked hard to give Carla everything they'd never had. They wanted so much for her—college, a good profession, happiness, and freedom from fear.

Although they called her their miracle child, raising her was difficult for them. When it became obvious that Carla was carrying a baby, they kept her home from school, and when she delivered in the summer, they didn't take her to a hospital but had a woman who delivered babies come to care for her through her time. And when the baby arrived—a boy was all they told Carla—the woman took him away and Carla never saw him again.

When she recovered, she was sent north to an aunt who lived in Brooklyn. They were just trying to protect her, Carla had said. What if whoever had done this to her came after her again? They were doing what they thought was right. They were too old by then to care for a child, and they never spoke to Carla about the baby or anything connected to that awful day again. It was as if it had never happened. The slate wiped clean.

So Carla put it out of her mind and grew up in Brooklyn and made a life for herself. But she never again let a man near her. Except for Raoul. He was her guardian. He would kill for her but she would never ask him to do that. There was no hatred in her heart. No fear or need for revenge. Just one regret. That she had never seen her son. So many years had passed and he had grown into a man by now. She had never spoken to him. Never said she was sorry for letting them take him from her.

And now, she might be able to find him, to know he was all right. That he had grown into a good man.

"That's her wish? To find the son that was taken away?" Joe let go of Alanna's arm. "Wow. How are we going to do that?"

"I don't know. She didn't wish for it yet. Only told me about what happened." Alanna's voice almost broke. "I can't believe anyone could go through what she's been through and . . ."

"What? Not feel rage about it?"

"Yes that. But also that she's become such a giving, caring person. Everyone seems to love her. Like Raoul. I could see it in his face. He'd lay down his life for her."

"Where's Morgan when we really need him? I guess we'd better get some rest and think hard about what we can do to make this wish a reality."

They spun off the barstools and once out on the sidewalk began to wander toward the bed and breakfast they'd found. Joe put his arm around Alanna's shoulders to comfort her. He stroked the hair away from her face so he could see her better. "Poor girl. This must have been hard for you to listen to all alone. I wish I had been there with you. But she wouldn't have talked with both of us there."

It was odd, this mix of life and not life. They seemed to have all the feelings of real live people and yet it was as if in some part of their souls they hovered above life, not quite feeling the brunt of it, not facing the same consequences as the living had to face. Alanna leaned her head against Joe's shoulder as they walked. He hugged her closer. There was a chilly wind, and the March air had a scent of an oncoming late-season snow. Alanna vaguely wished she and Joe were going home to their own house, to a life they truly shared. She caught the image—it was almost a wish and wasn't that an irony in itself—and stopped abruptly there on the sidewalk, half a block from the bed and breakfast.

"What is it?" Joe peered into her eyes.

"I just realized I miss something."

"What? Something from your old life?"

"I think so. I mean, I don't know if I miss him exactly. But I miss the feeling of belonging to someone. Of being with someone special. I wonder if he was the one. The way we left it before . . . " she didn't know what to call what had happened to them— "before Transition, my life was unfinished. I need to get back to finish it, because it's awfully cold out here."

Joe wrapped his arm around her again. "I think it's going to snow tonight. We'll be inside soon."

"I don't mean cold like the weather. I mean cold and alone."

"But we're together."

"Not really. You want to go back to life. And I want to go on to the next station, wherever that is. So we're just passing through Transition on our way to different places."

Chapter Eleven

Raoul stacked the last pan and stripped off his spattered apron. Raoul was particular about who did what at Carla's Home Cooking, preferring to let the wait staff handle the tables while he dealt with everything from ordering ingredients to preparing all the food they served. He chose the freshest ingredients from local producers, which meant that the menu varied from week to week and even day to day. You never knew exactly what was going to be on the menu, and that was one of main reasons people became regulars. So Raoul noticed anyone new who came in, and this week he'd seen a parade of new faces.

Everyone else had gone home long ago, but Carla sat at a table by the front window staring out at the street. Raoul noticed she had stopped figuring the receipts for the day before she'd gone through the whole stack. That was unusual. And after the white woman left, Carla hadn't moved.

"You gonna set there all night?" Raoul called from behind the bar, trying to sound playful, unconcerned, but he could tell something was not right and his own voice sounded a bit hollow. He'd had a bad feeling ever since that girl had been attacked back behind the restaurant. He'd had a bad feeling about something but he couldn't quite decide exactly what. All he knew was that Carla had been acting funny ever since it happened. Quiet. That wasn't like her. And as if she'd built a kind of invisible fence around herself. He couldn't get through it or around it, and this worried him.

He walked around the end of the bar. It wasn't a very long bar. Just big enough for eight people to sit and a few more to stand near the ones seated. Just a place to wait on a table being freed up. People didn't come to Carla's to get boozed up. They came for the food and the welcome atmosphere that Carla created. Raoul knew his personality wasn't the reason they came. But his food was the reason they came back.

"You hear me?"

"I hear you," Carla didn't move but kept gazing out the window.

In a moment Raoul slid into the seat opposite her at the booth.

"What'd that white lady want anyway?"

"She came back by to collect her wallet that slipped between that seat you just covered with your butt and the window over there at the wall."

"She find it?"

"Yes. She found it all right."

"Seem like she stayed here a might longer than she needed to just to collect her wallet. And seem like she and you got real chummy in the process. Seem like to me."

"I guess so."

"What you talk to her about?"

"Oh, just this and that and the other thing."

It seemed to Raoul that Carla had a faraway look in her eyes. like she was watching something happening on a TV screen only she could see.

"What other thing would that be now?"

But Carla sat quietly and didn't answer his question. Then she asked one of her own.

"Raoul, you got anything in your past you wished you could change? I mean if someone was to tell you they could let you have your wish and you could have anything? I mean within reason, you know."

"Within reason? How big a reason?"

Then she smiled. That's what Raoul could do. Make her smile when a smile was about as far away as it could get.

"Well, I guess big as you want. Not that you could change the past. But that you could catch up with it. Would you wish to do that?"

Raoul studied her. Whatever this was about and whoever that white lady was must be something powerful strong, he was thinking. Powerful strong. Like his last fight. The one when he knocked BoBo Taylor to the mat in the fifth round and BoBo never got back up again. The look on BoBo's face, with his lip cut and bleeding and his nose mashed into the mat and his muscled arm twisted to one side.

"Yeah," he said quietly. "I would change something in my past if I could wish for it to be different. Some things just stay with you forever. Like a tattoo on your soul."

Carla turned from the window, slowly facing Raoul. She held back the tears she could feel forming in her eyes. He reached out and laid his hand on hers. "It's gone be all right, you know. Nothing's so bad it can't be faced, and nothing in this world you can't face square on."

"They's things you don't know," she told him quietly. "Things nobody but me now living on this Earth knows. Things from the past that I put away deep in here." She touched her chest at the breastbone. "I don't know if I can survive with letting them out into the daylight. I just don't know."

They sat there like that, facing each other but not speaking any more. Raoul took his hand away. Whatever struggle was going on inside of Carla, he didn't press her about it. If she wanted to tell him, she would do it in her own time. He slid to the edge of the seat and stood up, touched the top button of his shirt as if he was checking to be sure it had not come loose on its own.

"You know I'm always here," he told her. "Always right here."

Carla looked up and smiled. "I know that, honeylamb. I do know that."

Chapter Twelve

It was one of those breezy March mornings, the sky a deep blue, as endless as the sea, a few buds, dark, red, bulging with new life on the spidery branches, slight eddies of wind picking up the old, fallen bits of leaves and whirling them around until they stopped scattering and lay in small piles here and there, contained by building walls or playground fences. A man in coveralls pushed a bin on wheels across one of a dozen kiddy parks scattered around the Brooklyn neighborhood. The man worked slowly. Raking, raking, raking, then lifting handfuls of leaves and dumping them into the bin on wheels he pushed along in front of him. He worked slowly, in no hurry to be done or to increase his collection rate.

A man and woman walking through the park past swings and climbing gyms looked like any other young couple from the neighborhood out on a late winter day. The bright sun warmed the air and their jackets were open, hands unfettered by gloves. But neither of them looked as if they were enjoying the first promise of spring, and they didn't seem to notice the pre-school children playing joyfully inside the playground.

"So what if she doesn't make the wish?" Alanna was saying to Joe. "How much time do we have anyway? It's been three days already."

"Relax. I'm sure Morgan would have told us if there was a time limit. Besides, what's your hurry? You have someplace important to be?"

There was irony in his voice and, of course, Alanna knew what he meant. Transition meant not worrying about where you were or how you got there or where you would be next. It was just the opposite of life. A kind of floating like you were in a fishbowl with no glass walls. Just swimming around from nowhere to anywhere. Yet still she felt this pull back to life.

"If this is the last wish we have to grant, yes, I'll be ready to go back. But to what?"

"You still amaze me. Here we are, free of all those earthly worries and struggles and yet you want to go back."

"What about you? Don't tell me you're not still trying to find out what happened to your partner, Russell. Don't tell me you've given up on finding his killer . . . on finding out why he was killed."

"Don't remind me. I know it's something that needs to be resolved. But not everything can find resolution. Not everything works out the way you want it to. No one knows that better than I do. I had twelve years in a courtroom to prove that you just can't predict where the chips are going to fall."

"But sometimes you do get an edge." The low, silken voice of Morgan drifted into their conversation, and as they looked around for him, all they saw was the rumpled worker wearing coveralls, raking leaves into a small pile. When he turned his head sideways and showed a sardonic little smile, Alanna and Joe realized who it was.

"Where have you been?" Joe scolded before Alanna could restrain him. "We're stuck with this one, you know. Can't get her to make the wish yet."

An enigmatic smile was all they got from Morgan. He bent over and picked up a stray branch but didn't toss it into the pushcart.

"What if this were a magic twig?" he asked quietly. "What would you do with it?"

Alanna and Joe looked at each other automatically as if they had just shared the exact same thought. Was Morgan adding a new wrinkle to their assignment? Was he offering them a chance at their own wish? Before they could say anything he spoke again.

"You see, for some people, a wish is always just at the very edge of their consciousness. They walk around on Earth wishing for everything they don't have. For them it's easy to make a wish. For them it's just a matter of deciding which one is the best wish at the time. But for some people a wish is so powerful, so potent, so filled with the possibility of pain and suffering, that they dare not hope to ask for it. On the other hand, the wish, for those people, is also so powerful in its redemptive potential that they cannot ignore it, no matter how they try to deny that it exists." He tossed the small branch into his cart and continued sweeping.

"You are the most frustrating individual," Alanna declared. As soon as the words were out of her mouth she regretted them. Morgan, after all, had enormous power over what happened to them. She never wanted to offend him. But Joe patted her on the shoulder as if to say "good girl," and when she looked at him he was grinning at her.

"It's not me who's frustrating you. You're doing it to yourself. You have the power. All you have to do is get her to turn her secret regret into a spoken wish." Morgan wandered away into the park then and kicked a ball that a small child had lost back into the playground. The child squealed with delight and toddled over to the ball.

Joe and Alanna looked away for a moment, confused by what he'd said. How in the world they could entice Carla into making her wish—without telling her beforehand that they could make it come true—appeared to be an insurmountable obstacle. When they turned to follow Morgan, to get more specific information out of him, he had evaporated like an eddy of wind leaving nothing but a few fallen leaves behind.

*

Detective Mathews thought about Carla all night long, even waking up from a dream about her sometime before sunrise. There was no sense in trying to go back to sleep when it had eluded him for so much of the night. So he rose early, showered, shaved, dressed, tucked his gun into the shoulder holster against his rib cage, and slid his arms into a gray wool jacket before grabbing his black trench coat and heading out to grab breakfast.

Lou Mathews had never married, although a long line of women had certainly used every wile imaginable to snare him into a permanent, legally binding arrangement. A couple of times he'd almost succumbed but had managed to back out before the final curtain fell. For the last few years, working undercover, he'd lived a semicelibate existence, with only a few meaningless flings between assignments. When he was working, it was just too dangerous for anyone to know much about him, even where he lived. Still, he was considered a catch. Tall, thick in the chest with big, sad eyes and a mellow voice that could melt snow off a sidewalk. But perhaps the one attribute that women found most alluring were his hands. Expressive and tender at the same time, his touch was enough to make a woman dissolve in his arms. It was not something he thought about or cultivated. But since he'd met Carla, he'd found his hands had an itchy sort of nervousness.

He was surprised at the impression Carla had made on him. She was decidedly not his type. At least not the type he'd been drawn to in the past. Or perhaps they'd been drawn to him and

60

it was easy for him to go along. Carla was what he considered a substantial woman. Not young anymore—but then neither was he. Not flashy. Not seductive. Not looking for a good time. Definitely not superficial. A woman you could talk to, confide in, share with—a woman to come home to after a long day. And there was something else. Although she came across as self-assured and stiff-spined, he sensed a vulnerable core, perhaps an old wound, and he wondered at the stories he'd heard about how she took people in. It was not a story he heard often in this city.

Detective Mathews found himself thinking these things and, at the same time, trying not to think about them. He was a man in conflict and he had no idea why, all of a sudden, this woman had struck so deep a chord. He was even considering asking her out. He shook his head at the thought. He must be slipping. He decided he would go to a local cop bar after work and submerge these strange stirrings in a few scotch and waters. But that was later. Now he turned the corner and headed down Court Street straight for Carla's Home Cooking. Well, he did need breakfast. And he'd heard great things about her food. And there were a few details he needed to get straightened out about this girl, Tempest.

Chapter Thirteen

Destiny was less upset about the alley attack than Carla seemed to be. In fact, everyone was making a big deal about it and Tempest just wanted to get on with her life—such as it was. She allowed Carla to fuss over her because it meant a well-heated, albeit small, room upstairs in the back of the big old house with a large backyard and that odd man and his dog on the floor below. And there was always good food in the refrigerator or simmering on the stove. Carla was out from morning until night, and that left Tempest with plenty of time to think and plan.

Her first step was to get a job. She could have subbed for the waitresses at Carla's, but she didn't want everyone watching her. So she canvassed the neighborhood and picked up a full-time gig at Doyle's, a bar that also served Irish food, a few blocks from the house. An easy walk. And night hours. A good excuse to be out. The scratches and bruises began to heal, and she wore long sleeves and leggings to cover them. With her first paycheck, she invested in a low-cut, tight-fitting top and a sleek pair of red heels. Tips came easily, and within two days she was pulling in a nice salary. She always encouraged the male customers to tip in cash. Said she needed the cab fare to get home to Queens, that riding the subway at night was too dangerous, or whatever story came to her in the moment. When she was working one of them, she'd lean forward to show more cleavage. The distraction always worked. Men were a dumb bunch, she thought, and nothing she'd experienced so far had disabused her of this opinion.

Each night when she clocked out, there was always at least one well-oiled straggler hanging around to hook up with her.

But these were easy marks not up to her tricks, and she always brushed them off with ease. Once or twice she wondered what Carla would do or say if she knew just who she'd invited into her home. But Tempest shrugged these thoughts off as easily as she brushed away the barflies. She had neither time nor inclination for idle entanglements or emotional connections. Her mission was clear and she was single-minded in her pursuit of it.

She chose her job carefully at a place where she felt right at home. Doyle's featured a suggestive painting of a woman lying on some hay bales inside a horse barn. One of her stocking-clad legs hung over the side of a bale, and her foot was encased in a type of shoe that no woman would ever have worn into a barn. She was gazing intently up at a rack of rifles hanging on a wall above her, and to one side a line of whips hung vertically from a series of brass hooks. If one studied the painting closely, the hooks were actually small animal sculptures—a fox, a bear, a panther, a snake, and a hawk. And if one took a magnifying glass to the painting to look especially closely at the animals, one would notice that all the beasts had fangs and that the hooks that held the whips were actually long claws.

Beneath the painting, row upon row of bottles featuring every type of alcohol lined cascading shelves. The bar itself had been carved out of a single massive slab of marble decades before, perhaps even a century ago, its edges worn soft, its surface scuffed and dipped in places where hands had rubbed it and glasses had been shoved across its surface over and over.

The bar had a long history. Cops and criminals alike had been patrons for as long as anyone could remember. The original Doyle had long ago passed on, and a series of Doyle brothers, sons, cousins, and grandsons had taken over. Currently the bar was under the watchful eye of Michael Doyle, who had his fingers submerged in more than one cask of Irish whiskey. Word had it that Michael D, as he was known, dealt in a variety of contraband, and if you couldn't buy what you wanted directly from Michael D, he could point you in the right direction—for a cut, of course.

Thus it was a double irony that not only criminals and cops kicked back together but that the second time Detective Mathews and Tempest crossed paths, it would be at Doyle's, late at night, when the cop and the crime victim were both in search of something. But not the same thing.

*

Joe hooked his arm through Alanna's and hugged her rather close as they headed back to Carla's Home Cooking. They hoped for a divine revelation before they reached the front door, something that would give them a clue to unlock Carla's wish. Joe found the slight pressure of Alanna's hip against his quite pleasant. He wondered what it meant to her.

"So," he whispered into her ear. "Here we are again. Just like the old days."

Alanna leaned her face away from him to stare him down. "What old days?"

He pulled her back into position. "In Vegas. Remember? At the chapel, just as the ceremony ended and we were this close." He brushed her cheek with his lips. "Just a kiss apart and then we dematerialized and Morgan pulled us back."

"Morgan," Alanna muttered. "He drives me crazy. Why can't he just tell us how to get Carla's wish? Why does he have to make it such a mystery?"

Joe frowned. He had a different mystery on his mind.

"Listen," he whispered close to her ear again, so close she could feel his warm breath. "Tonight, when the B & B is all asleep, how about I pad on over to your room for a visit?" He bumped her hip on purpose and let their thighs rub against each other.

Alanna stopped dead in her tracks. "We're on a mission here," she scolded him.

"I know that very well. But the mission doesn't have to be so single-minded that we don't do anything else. It could be a double mission." He slid his arm around her waist and they started walking again. "I don't think Morgan cares what we do together as long as we get the wish done."

"You're terrible," she said but she giggled, and Joe took that as encouragement. He pulled her into a deep, recessed doorway and backed against the glass doors until the doors parted, allowing the couple to fall into the small, empty lobby of what appeared to be a professional building. Joe pulled her over to a side wall away from the entrance and tilted her head back with his index finger under her chin. He'd been wanting to do this for what seemed like an eternity, and in their case, maybe it actually had been an eternity. They had no way of knowing how much time had passed since they'd been in Transition or how much longer they would be stuck there. So he kissed her. Gently at first, testing her response, his hands lightly on her shoulders, which were covered by a thin wool coat. But his hands quickly moved down to the buttons and worked them open so his fingers could explore farther down, beneath the coat, beneath the blouse, down to her skin and the bra that covered her breasts. He kissed her until he felt her shoulders go limp and her arms wound around him.

"Joe," she murmured. "What if we get into trouble? What if Morgan finds out?"

"Forget Morgan," he whispered and kissed her silent.

Her eyes closed but Joe kept his open, for he wanted to know how Alanna would respond to him, to look for clues before he pushed any further. And because his eyes were open, he saw in the reflection in the glass doors a blonde woman rush by on the street. And he suddenly stopped kissing Alanna and spun around to be sure of what he'd seen. He pulled her by the hand, back toward the glass doors, to look out onto the sidewalk as the blonde woman walked quickly in the opposite direction.

"You go on to Carla's," he told her quickly. "I've got to find out about something. I'll catch up with you later. For sure." He squeezed her butt before he pulled open the glass door and ran toward the woman who was disappearing down the street, swallowed by the sudden crush of people breaking for a Brooklyn lunch.

Alanna let out a slow breath. She felt excited and deflated at the same time. Is this what it would be like with Joe? Heightened expectation followed by a big letdown was not her idea of . . . of what? She was confused. This was not the time or place to be indulging their passions. Or thinking about sex or anything beyond it. Not until she was sure of her next step. And nothing was sure about that.

*

Carla's was packed. Alanna spotted one empty seat at the bar. She'd considered dematerializing so she could hang around unseen but then wondered what good that would have done her. She needed to get Carla talking again, so she'd just have to stall until the busy lunch hour was over. She came up with a plan and luckily, because she'd arrived so late, it took longer than usual to order and get her food. By the time she was served the lobster bisque and spinach-shiitake mini quiche she'd ordered, people were paying their tabs and heading back to work.

Good, she thought as she took the first sip of soup, that'll give me time to engage Carla again. And then her eyebrows shot up as the slightly piquant flavor of the lobster bisque hit her taste buds. Wow, this is really good, she thought and wolfed it down. Long gone were her first meals in Transition. The not-drinks that had kept them going with their strange energizing effect. The not-drinks Morgan had served them as a none too well disguised bartender. They hadn't had a not-drink in ages it seemed. Morgan wasn't around so much lately. Alanna shrugged. Oh, well, perhaps they were well on their wish-granter way by now and didn't need as much hand-holding.

"You like that?" It was Carla at her elbow.

"Mmm-hmm," Alanna answered and swallowed the last spoonful. "Really incredible. You know—" and this had been her plan but here Carla was almost offering herself up to it— "I'd love to ask about some of your recipes. Everything is so delicious. I've had lobster bisque before but it never tasted this good."

"Honey, I can tell you one thing about this bisque. We use a special wine and we always use fresh cream from the farmers. And then Raoul, when he took over the cooking from me, he added something else that he won't tell a soul. Not even me. Says that's job security." Carla laughed, and her eyes crinkled with pleasure.

Alanna took a forkful of quiche and practically hummed as it melted in her mouth, more like a pastry than a main course.

"This is fabulous, too," she smiled at Carla. "I enjoyed talking with you last night."

"Listening to me more like." Carla slid onto the bar chair next to Alanna. "I thank you for listening. Sometimes it's easier to talk to a stranger. Sometimes you're likely to tell a stranger something that's been deep down here," she pointed to her heart, "so long it's gotten stuck there."

"I had the feeling that you had something more to say. Maybe something you wanted that you thought maybe saying it out loud might—I don't know—put a curse on it or something." Alanna thought that sounded lame and would never get Carla to make the wish.

"It's funny you say that," Carla's voice dropped to almost a whisper. "Because all night long and all day since I woke up, I've been feeling I wanted to do something. I can't for life the of me think why. Maybe it's all the goings-on lately. That girl getting attacked, reminding me of what happened. Maybe I'm just getting older and afraid that if I don't make up for what happened pretty soon now, I never will."

Alanna reached over and touched Carla's wrist ever so slightly. "Go ahead. Speak it out loud. To me. I'm sure it will help you."

Carla didn't move her hand away. Instead she placed her own hand over Alanna's and looked into her eyes as if she was trying to read something in them, some message, or find some certainty there. When she finally released her hand and looked away it was with a deep sigh, and when she looked back at Alanna, it happened.

68

"I wish I could find my boy. 'Course he would be a man now. I wish I could find him and let him know his real mama has never stopped thinking about him. Never. Not for one day."

Chapter Fourteen

Doyle's was half empty, which also meant it was half full. In the middle of the day, this was unusual for a Brooklyn bar. But this was not your usual hipster/yuppie pub, although they also frequented Doyle's, just not at this time of day. They showed up on Friday nights and Saturdays. In the middle of the week, in the middle of the day, there was business being conducted at Doyle's.

Joe followed the blonde woman as closely as he felt he could without being spotted. He couldn't duck into a side street and dematerialize until he knew where she would land. But when he saw her pull the big brass handle on the door at Doyle's, he did look around for somewhere safe to fade unnoticed. He found a spot across the street from Doyle's in a short space that looked like an old pathway between two buildings that had been half built over long ago. It was hard to imagine it now, but Brooklyn had once been farms and streams and mooing cows. Now it was all young marrieds with babies and toddlers, professional Wall Street types and artists and writers who'd migrated from Manhattan where condo and coop prices had squeezed out all but the super rich. Where he was standing had been a slum fifty years ago. Fifty years before that, a farm. And a hundred years before that, wild flowers along the banks of the Gowanus Inlet, a series of tidal creeks fed by a saltwater marshland.

Joe hunched against a wall and took a deep breath. It had been a while since he'd tried The Manifest, but he was pretty sure it would work. And it did. He evaporated and landed inside Doyle's. The Manifest was perhaps the coolest thing about Transition. This ability to wander without form, to disappear and appear somewhere else almost instantaneously. To overhear conversations and observe without being seen. He would miss that when he returned to life.

If only he could have done that before the car crash and his own semi-demise, he'd still be trying cases and maybe his partner, Russ, would still be alive. What he could have done with that in the courtroom. Instead here he was, invisible for the moment, spying on his partner's widow—the blonde woman—trying to figure out what had happened to poor, clueless Russ.

He spotted her seated at a back booth in semidarkness opposite a man of about fifty. It was hard to see details about him in this light, but Joe did get a good look at big, thick fingers wrapped around a frothy beer mug, a heavy ring on one pinky. This was the kind of guy he sometimes met up with in a police station interrogation room just after he'd been called to represent someone who refused to talk to the cops. It was the kind of guy he would have met once and then referred to Russ. Thug types were Russell's meat and potatoes. And sometimes he almost got paid in meat and potatoes. Unless the guy was connected. And then the rewards could be sweet.

From what Joe could gather from their conversation, Elaine—that was Russell's widow's name—wanted something back. She called him Benny and he wanted—there it was—more money or something else. They argued and Elaine sank back against the booth looking discouraged. But not for long. She leaned in, her eyes squinty, and she twirled a lock of blonde hair between her fingers.

So that was it. Joe had never liked Elaine. No, he thought, it wasn't that he didn't like her. He just never trusted her. He hovered just behind them in an empty booth. He had to turn so he could hear what they said.

"I know you got a real nice insurance settlement." That was Benny Fingers. "Someone told me it was a couple million bucks. Now, I don't wanna be greedy, but I think what I done was worth more than what you paid. Now that gun. The one you supplied. That gun has some telltale prints on it. And they ain't mine. So I assume you want that gun back so you can—how would you say—dispose of it permanently?"

"Look," Elaine could be very persuasive. Joe knew that. Hadn't she tried to persuade him a couple of times when Russ was out of town? She'd been a Vegas showgirl and she still had all the right equipment. It was what got Russ interested in the beginning. And Elaine wanted to get off the stage and out of that life. So she worked on Russ and it wasn't long before he capitulated. Joe remembered how proud he'd been, how he'd shown Joe her pictures. Russ had taken plenty of pictures. He'd shown them off all over Boston. Now here she was in Brooklyn. She must have come down here to find someone to do the job, Joe figured, and found Benny Fingers.

Elaine reached across the table and touched one of those fingers with her thumb. She ran along it until she got to his hand and them moved up to his wrist. Benny smiled and grabbed her hand and held it tight.

"I tell you what, lady. I can buy what I want. But maybe you and me, we can do some more nice business. But first, you just get that money together and meet me here in three days and we'll trade. Then we can talk about our future plans." He pushed the beer mug aside and slid out of the booth. He waved to Doyle, who was seated at a table playing rummy with someone. Doyle nodded and continued his game, but he watched Fingers leave the bar and noted that Elaine stayed behind.

72

So did Joe, who decided now would be a good time to reverse The Manifest. He reappeared in the men's room and regained bodily form. This is getting easier, he thought, and smiled at himself in the cracked mirror above the sink. Maybe it wouldn't be so bad to stay in Transition for eternity, he reasoned. It had its advantages. Except for Alanna.

He really wanted to have some earthly contact with her. In fact, those feelings were getting stronger all the time, and he wondered if that meant they were supposed to get together, even if he was going to be moving on and she was staying up there. It was a confused situation at this point but one thing was sure, he thought, seeing Russ get shot was no bad dream. It had really happened. Now to find out why and how, although he had a strong feeling about that, too.

He sauntered out of the men's room with such a chip on his shoulder that if he'd met a drunk, he was sure he could deck him with one punch and laugh while doing it. Decking Elaine was another matter. He couldn't sucker punch her, and he wasn't sure that showing his hand at this point would be a great idea. And then there was the problem of Morgan. If Joe went so far off course as to reveal himself to Elaine while he was also about to make his move on Alanna, surely Morgan would step in and then the consequences might be—well, he wondered what they would be. Morgan had never actually told them about punishments, but in the back of his mind, Joe remembered his Catholic schooling. Hell was nowhere to spend eternity.

Elaine had ordered another couple of rounds of whatever she'd been drinking, and Joe made his way to the bar so he could surreptitiously watch her.

"Not a good idea, Joe," the bartender told him softly.

Joe swiveled around to face Morgan, who was wiping a tall glass he'd just washed.

"What isn't?"

"Funny, I thought you'd be the one I didn't have to watch. You being a lawyer and all. You know there are rules. You know they have to be followed or you have to take the consequences."

"You make the rules?" Joe raised his eyebrows, taunting Morgan.

Morgan chuckled. "The rules are there, Joe. I don't make them. They just exist. You're here to grant a wish. Not to get revenge."

"But he was my partner."

Morgan chuckled again. "You think you're Bogey and this is *The Maltese Falcon?* Wise up, Joe. Your partner got mixed up in some nasty business. Very nasty. Nastier than even his wife knew. But she's not exactly a clean slate, either."

"And I'm supposed to sit back and do nothing? Let his death go unavenged?"

Morgan set a beer down in front of Joe. "On the house," he said and waited until Joe sucked off the foam and downed half the glass. "Better?" he asked.

Joe nodded and then tilted his head slightly. "That wasn't beer."

Morgan smiled and Joe realized it was one of those not-drinks from the very first time he'd met Morgan at a bar. He'd been with Alanna that time, and they'd had not-drinks together and both felt fantastic after their drinks.

"So you're telling me to let her go? Just walk away and do nothing, is that it?"

"These things have a way of working themselves out, Joe. That is, if you stick to your plan and follow the rules." Morgan shrugged his shoulders and refilled Joe's glass. "Of course, if you don't follow the rules, I can't guarantee anything."

Chapter Fifteen

Now that Carla had spoken her wish out loud, Alanna could tell her everything. This was when she needed Joe to be there. To back her up. She knew Carla would never believe her and would want proof or some way to verify that they were wish granters. Convincing Carla was going to be the first hurdle. And then granting the wish would be the next. Alanna knew that granting a wish was only the beginning. Carla would soon face a series of tough decisions along the way. That's why there was that old saying "Be careful what you wish for." So where was Joe?

And boom, there he was, walking through the door, and Alanna's heart thumped and she thought, what's this now. I feel like a teenager all of a sudden. He's got me wondering where he is and who he's talking to. This is ridiculous. One kiss and I start to disintegrate. I've got to keep my head on straight. We have a mission and this is where it gets sticky.

Watching Joe saunter in, his shoulders squared, sure of himself and moving gracefully like an athlete, with that little gleam in his eye when his gaze met hers, well, it was going to be tough to concentrate on the wish. And Alanna also noticed a certain air about Joe that she hadn't seen since—when had she last seen it—oh, yes, when they'd had those not-drinks and they'd both felt kind of exhilarated and light-headed and really wonderful. Alanna turned quickly to Carla, who was still dazed by her own admission that she wished she could find her son after all these years.

"Carla," she began softly, "my, um, my partner, Joe, is going to join us in a minute. And we have something to tell you.

Something really important. Maybe we should go sit in a booth in the back where we won't be disturbed."

Carla just looked at her, not understanding, or perhaps not capable of thinking about much of anything right then. It was unusual for Carla not to be in the driver's seat.

"Come on," Alanna gently took Carla by the arm and led her away to a booth while Joe quickly switched direction to join them. "Come, sit down here."

She helped Carla into the booth and sat beside her with Joe sliding in opposite the two of them. They had her boxed in now. This was best, Alanna thought. Carla would have to hear them out. None of them noticed Raoul step out of the kitchen, untie his apron, and stand behind the counter with his arms crossed over his chest, biceps flexed. From there he had a clear sight line to their booth.

And suddenly there he was, with three coffee mugs held by his thumb and fingers in one hand, and a pot of fresh coffee in the other. He set the mugs down rather harshly, Alanna thought, before he said, "Coffee for all three?" He glared at Joe and stared at Alanna. She thought it best to placate him. If he stayed, they couldn't talk to Carla about the wish.

"Thank you. That would be perfect. Carla's just about to give me some recipe advice. Maybe you'd like to share your secret ingredient for that lobster bisque?"

That did it. Raoul turned and disappeared back into the kitchen without saying another word. Joe winked at Alanna as if to say, "Well done, girl." Then he turned to Carla.

""I'm Joe," he said. "I was here the other day with Alanna. You might not remember me."

"I remember you, sugar." Carla smiled at him but it wasn't her usual full-on-charm-the-people smile. It was wary and a bit confused. In truth, she felt uncomfortable being wedged in like

76

this, and she squirmed in her seat. She was wearing a silk blouse with a ruffled scoop neck, and Joe could see the effects of her heart beating harder than usual, causing the ruffles to fan at the edges.

"Good." Joe stated it definitely, as if he was leading a client through the steps of a trial. One step at a time. Make sure the client was with him at every step, let the client know that everything was going exactly as it should. "Because Alanna and I—well, Alanna and I did not stumble into your restaurant by accident."

"That's right," Alanna liked the way Joe was leading up to this. She felt more relaxed now that he was here. And, at the same time, she felt more on edge. That kiss. It had done something to her, changed something.

"We know this is going to seem strange to you. And you're right to think it is, but I assure you, what we're about to tell you is the absolute truth."

"What are you two not saying with all this talk?" Carla looked from Joe to Alanna and back to Joe. "Does this have something to do with that girl? Tempest? Because she's safe at my house and I'm watching over her. Nobody going to do nothing to that girl again." She reverted to a kind of vernacular that she almost never used. Unless she was stressed and feeling defensive and aggressive at the same time.

"No," Joe shook his head slowly, calmly. "It's not about her. It's about you."

"About what you told me when we were sitting at the counter. Remember?" Alanna placed her fingers softly on Carla's hand. "About your son. About how you've never stopped thinking about him, about how you wished you could find him. We're here to make that wish come true for you."

"That's very sweet of you two strangers to be concerned about me. Now being a city girl for so long a time now, I've been accustomed to all sorts of folks coming in here and telling me all sorts of tales. You'd be surprised by some of them, as I've been at times." Carla took a deep breath as if she'd been running up a set of stairs. "And I know that my place here has become a refuge for some and a gathering place for others. I know this neighborhood and the people in it like the back of my hand. But I also know that some things can't be fixed. No way. No how. So even though I do thank you for your concern, I think this has gone as far as it's going to go and I'll just take myself out of here, if you don't mind."

"Stay put, Carla," Joe told her in a quiet voice, the voice he used to use for criminals he figured were guilty but who he'd defend, sometimes for a lot of money, sometimes because he felt they needed his help, sometimes just to see if he could win the game.

Chapter Sixteen

Detective Mathews took a long sip of beer while two off-duties—one tall, the other short—sitting next to him at the bar yammered on about the Knicks. One of them had a bet against the weekend game and the other one was telling him it was a sucker bet, that the Knicks were sure to win. They started arguing about the odds until finally Mathews turned to them and asked, "Either of you guys know what scam Doyle's got going on these days?"

They may have been off duty and a little loaded, but they were not about to spill their guts without knowing why. They stared at Detective Mathews and stalled by taking another drink. One of them, the taller one, motioned to the bartender for another round.

"You're Mathews, from the one seven, right?"

Mathews nodded but was otherwise impassive.

"Why you want to know about Doyle?"

Mathews shrugged. Maybe they thought he was a spy from Internal Affairs, sniffing around for dirt on other cops.

"What're you working on?" the shorter one asked as the drinks arrived. He shoved the empty glasses toward the bartender, who whisked them away. Drinkers don't like reminders of how many they've already had. They like to look to the future as if it were a blank page ready to fill.

"Nothing much," Mathews evaded. "You guys hear what happened out behind Carla's the other night?"

Taller cop snorted. "From what I hear the perp didn't get very far."

Shorter cop laughed at that. "I suppose you'd have finished the job?"

"Damn right. If I was in her position." They both howled at that and drank some more.

"Any rumors on who the guy was?"

"Nah," Taller cop had settled down. "Haven't heard much at all. Just some rumbling that he mighta been from out of town. But that's just talk around the house, you know."

"I know how it is," Mathews nodded. "So Doyle . . . think he might know anything about it?"

Now taller cop leaned in to Mathews so no one could overhear what they were talking about. "If I were you, I'd keep questions about Doyle to yourself."

"And why is that?"

Shorter cop grunted. "Doyle's connected."

"I know," Mathews agreed. "Anyway, he'd have to be."

"No, no, you don't understand. He's connected every which way a guy can be connected. His fingers are in every pie you can imagine but he's clean, as far as we can tell. I'm just saying I'd watch my step where Doyle's concerned if I were you. He's got a guardian angel somewhere. Maybe at city hall."

Mathews knew some of this already. After all, if you were going to find out what was going on with criminals, you had to hang out with criminals. That's why Doyle's was so popular with both sides. They had to know who was watching who, when, and where. Doyle never seemed to get too involved, always sitting at one of the back tables playing rummy or hearts. Word was he never bet on anything, never even played poker, that he made his money from the bar and had nothing on the side. Except information.

"So he's just your average Honest Joe citizen, huh?"

Taller cop shrugged one shoulder. "I hear he's helped crack cases. And I also hear he's helped get some sidelined indefinitely. Why? You got one has you stumped? Some sweet little thing got her panties in a wad?" The two laughed again but this time nervously. "It's not like you're sex crimes anyway."

They went back to their drinks and Mathews looked down at what was left in his beer mug. "Yeah, her panties got wadded up real tight, boys," he said softly, almost to himself. "But I don't think that's all there is. So maybe Doyle knows something. Worth a shot. I think I'll go over and sit in on his game."

*

Michael Doyle dressed like a gentleman. His hair was neatly clipped, fingernails buffed and trimmed evenly, red striped silk tie held in place with a thin gold tie clip, an expensively tailored custom suit, and a monogrammed shirt with French cuffs. Michael Doyle looked as if he should and could have been lunching at the Four Seasons or the Yale Club with Wall Street corporate attorneys, but here he was sitting at a back table playing an average hand of gin with a guy who looked like he should and could be unloading some flat screens that had "fallen" off the back of a truck.

Neither of the men said a word when Detective Mathews walked over to their table. Except that Michael said "gin" quietly and laid his cards open on the table. Three fours, three kings, and the nine, ten, jack, and queen of clubs. He made a note on a little pad by his elbow. "That makes my game." He looked up at Detective Mathews. "You play?" he asked.

"Sure," Mathews pulled out a chair. "Stakes?"

"No stakes," Michael shuffled. "Just a friendly game. You win, I'll owe you a favor. I win, you'll owe me one. Neighborly." He dealt the cards and nodded to his former partner, who pushed his chair back and wandered off slightly disconcerted, it seemed to Detective Mathews.

"Hope I didn't interrupt," he said as he picked up his cards and wondered if the deck was marked. He was not a card player and wouldn't know how to spot a marked deck.

"You want me to crack open a new deck and deal a fresh hand?" Doyle asked, smiling.

"I trust you," Mathews answered and picked up the discard. He reorganized his hand. "My mother played cards," he offered. "She used to cheat. Made me cautious."

"Huh," Doyle grunted and picked a fresh card from the top of the deck. He discarded and looked at Mathews with his chin pointed down and his eyes looking up from under furrowed brows. "You used to work vice." It was not a question. "Over in the city."

"Yeah." Mathews discarded. "I got reassigned to Brooklyn a while back. To major crime."

"What're you doing in here? Just stopped in for a quick beer?" Doyle picked up the discard and slipped it into the middle of his hand.

"Actually," Mathews picked a new card and studied his hand. "I came in to talk to you."

Doyle's eyebrows shot up as Mathews discarded.

"What about?" Doyle picked a new card and discarded.

"I think you know," Mathews picked up the discard and looked at it and then at his hand. "About that rape the other night."

"I heard it was an attack and maybe not a rape."

"You heard wrong."

"I never hear wrong," Doyle's voice was so low Mathews had to lean in to hear what he said.

"So I understand." Mathews collapsed his cards and held them in his hand. "So what does that mean? A girl was attacked. She says she was raped. And you say she wasn't. You weren't there. So how would you know?"

Doyle collapsed his cards and they both stared at each other. "Suppose I was to tell you a story?"

"Okay. What kind of a story?"

"The kind that doesn't make sense."

"Go ahead. I'm listening."

Chapter Seventeen

"You two are talking crazy," Carla looked from Alanna to Joe and back. "I never heard of anything so . . ." She couldn't find words to characterize it. "What do you really want?"

Joe smiled and Alanna took a deep breath. This was going to be even harder than she'd anticipated.

"It's true, Carla," Alanna assured her. "Trust us and you'll see. We've done this twice already and I can assure you—"

Joe interrupted. "Look, Carla, I understand this is a tough concept to grasp and accept. Believe me, it was difficult for us in the beginning, too. Just imagine—"

Alanna interrupted Joe. No sense in telling their whole story to poor Carla, who was already so confused. "Here's what Joe is trying to say. You just go about your normal daily routine and you'll see, we'll make this wish happen. Of course, what you do with it is up to you."

Carla stared at her, dumbstruck now. "You mean, it's really true? Like winning the lottery or getting your dream house or something? What's going to happen? Are you going to cast some sort of spell and make my son appear in front of me?" A frightened look crossed her face for an instant. "You're not . . ." but she didn't finish the sentence.

"No, no, no, we're not anything bad. We're not devils or witches or anything like that." Alanna shook her head vehemently.

"But if you were, you wouldn't tell me you were. You'd say you were something else. Something good and nice." She tilted her head, suspicion written all over her face.

"You don't even believe in the Devil," Joe muttered.

84

"How you know that?"

"I just know. And I also know that you want to accept this. Think of it as a gift because you've helped so many other people. Think of it as something just for you. Especially for you because you're special."

"I'm not special," Carla murmured. "I have so much, and so many others deserve so much more."

It was a typical response, and Alanna was ready for it. "Even if you think you're not special or that others deserve their wish more than you do, our being here refutes that. And you have no choice. You have to accept what we're offering you. You can't wish it for someone else. It doesn't work that way."

Carla saw that it was no use arguing. Okay, she thought, so they say they'll grant my wish, and that alone is crazy, but how are they going to find my son? I have no idea what happened to that baby. He could be anywhere now. He could be on the moon for all I know . . . A feeling of loss overwhelmed her and her head sank down so that she seemed shorter suddenly.

"All right," Carla held up her hands in a helpless gesture. "All right. I agree. You're going to grant my wish. Crazy as that sounds. But how do you do that? How do you find him?"

*

"One day, from out of the blue, a guy shows up at my bar." Doyle had folded his cards on the table, interrupting their rummy game. "Nobody knows who he is, but word is he's from out of town. So I make inquiries and ask a few people to nose around. Because this guy looks like bad news to me."

85

Detective Mathews held onto his cards but collapsed them so they were just a small stack. He leaned forward to hear because Doyle was talking so low. One finger tapped the table softly. It was a nervous habit whenever he was thinking. He didn't ask why the guy looked like bad news, figuring Doyle was not the sort to embellish. Bad news takes lots of forms, Mathews figured, but they can all lead to the same end result. So he listened.

"Play the hand," Doyle told him, so Mathews fanned open his cards and picked a new one, then discarded.

"This guy had no past that anyone could tell. It was like he showed up from outer space. That never happens. Not in my place. Somebody shows up here, I figure they're here for a reason and somebody from somewhere sent them. But this guy, he sits at the bar and watches people come and go for about a week. Then he disappears for a week and shows up again the other night a couple hours before your attack."

"My attack?" Mathews raised his eyebrows.

"So-called rape." Doyle continued. "Now you tell me why a guy from nowhere comes in here, hangs around talking to no one, just watching, then disappears, reappears, and shows up again after there's this story of a rape out behind Carla's. And I tell you what, his head has been bashed on the side and he's dripping blood down his neck and onto his jacket. He looks like he's been in a helluva brawl. Well, I don't ask people anything unless they talk first, so I let it go. He has a few drinks and then slinks outta here. It wasn't 'til a few days later I hear Carla had clubbed the guy when she caught him in the act. And then I put two and two together and came up with five."

"So? What are you saying?"

"I'm not finished," Doyle picked up his cards, looked at his hand and then at the discard pile, picked up the next card from the deck, and laid out his hand. "Gin," he said. "Now you owe me a favor. But I'm going to give you this one, because that guy is up to some kinda no good and what it is gives me the willies."

"Well, I guess I'll owe you one," Mathews frowned, wondering where Doyle was going with this.

"The night after the attack, late, way after midnight, the girl shows up in here. She goes over to that back booth and pretty soon in comes the guy and slides in next to her. He's cleaned up by then, with a bandage on his head and different clothes. Real cozy, the two of them. Hands all over each other. If that was rape, then I'm the Pope." Doyle leaned back again.

"Hmmm," Mathews mused. He didn't know how this fit into his investigation, but it was certainly interesting information. Still, it was just a story without facts. Proof, that's what he needed. But he wouldn't find it here.

"Now, what have you got for me?" Doyle's eyes narrowed. His was a reciprocal world, and it was Mathews' turn to give up something.

Mathews tilted his head to one side. "I can't really divulge much, but I can tell you this. Your guy is a mystery. You're right about that. But he does have a past. It's a bit fuzzy. Did you see a blonde woman in here earlier? Probably sitting with that same man who didn't look like the kind of man she should be sitting with?"

"I saw her," Doyle nodded.

"She has a past, too," was all Mathews told him, and Doyle was left to start matching up puzzle pieces in his head, which is exactly what Detective Mathews had been trying to do ever since a truck crashed into Joe's car on a clear morning and sent Joe flying into Transition.

Chapter Eighteen

"How *are* we going to find him?" Alanna asked Joe.

They'd walked out of Carla's without answering her questions, but it seemed to Alanna they had left her in an okay place, at least as okay as anyone could be who needs time to process this kind of news. They'd told her to be patient, that it wouldn't take long, which at first only heightened her general sense that her life had suddenly tilted and she was sliding down a chute to the unknown. But she recovered her equilibrium before they left and said she would try not to—as she said—"melt away." Alanna thought of an ice cube in the hot sun, but she didn't see Carla as a wilting flower, so she smiled at her and patted her arm reassuringly. It was one of those moments when Joe was completely out of his element, and he stood up abruptly as if he'd been poked.

Now, out on the street, he took Alanna's arm and steered her away from the restaurant.

"Let's go back to the B & B," he pulled her to his side. "We've done enough today. We can start searching for her son later." He leaned down and brushed her cheek with his lips. Her hair smelled like some flower from his childhood—lilac, maybe? He vaguely remembered an old lilac tree outside his bedroom window. He'd climbed down it once when his mother had told him to stay in his room all afternoon after he'd lied abut something and she'd caught him in the lie. What he'd lied about was long forgotten but he remembered raising the window as quietly as possible, inch by inch, and prying the screen out so he could reach the main branches of the tree. It was in full boom and the scent of those lavender blossoms had surrounded him like a fog, but the branches were not strong enough to support him. When one snapped, he lost his footing, slid down and down, breaking more branches as he went until he landed on the hard ground, his arms scraped and his calf twisted at an odd angle. He didn't realize it was broken and had to drag himself back to the front door and try to sneak up to his room. Of course his mother heard the door and came running. If his leg hadn't been broken, she would have walloped him for sure, but his sorry state won her over. And through it all the scent of lilacs stayed with him.

He breathed in deeply and hugged Alanna closer so that their hips moved as one as they walked down the street in perfect sync. She leaned her head into his neck without resistance as he steered them toward the B & B where they'd somehow managed to land after The Manifest had transported them back to Earth.

"Joe," Alanna whispered into his ear so no one else could hear, but who would have been listening in the street anyway? "What are we doing? Aren't you worried that Morgan will find out?"

He nuzzled her neck. "I told you before what I thought about that. And I can't wait any longer."

He squeezed her arm and his hand brushed against her breast. Alanna felt a jolt run through her body. It seemed like an eternity since a man had touched her. Maybe it had been. There was no way to tell how much time had passed since she left her life on Earth behind. The cars all looked the same. The stores were selling the same brands. She assumed they had lost only a little time, and the sooner she could finish up their assignment . . . well, she was in a hurry to sort things out, but now she was here. With Joe. It couldn't be wrong to give in to her feelings.

Their pace quickened. Alanna felt the muscles in Joe's arm stiffen. One more block and they'd be at their temporary home. His hand moved up to the back of her neck and he rubbed her skin. A tingling sensation moved down her spine and somewhere below her stomach a feeling of pressure began to build. She turned her head to see Joe's face. He was staring at her, his eyes bright, mouth slightly open.

"I want to kiss you," he said. "And see you naked."

At that moment a man dressed in ragged clothes, holding a soiled Starbuck's cup stepped out from the curb directly in front of them, pulling them up short, and they released from each other's arms.

"Spare some change?" his voice was gruff as he held out the cup and shuffled between them, and it was at that moment they saw who he was.

"Morgan," Joe said.

"Going somewhere?" Morgan asked in that low gravelly voice of his, and grinned.

Alanna looked down at the sidewalk as if she'd been stopped by a traffic cop. She blushed a deep red and finally glanced up to see what punishment Morgan had in mind. He just grinned at them and jiggled the change in his cup.

"Generous folks here in Brooklyn," he told them. "I'd like to stay here awhile and get to know more of them. But, like you two, I have an assignment and can't be using valuable time on nonessential tasks, no matter how pleasant."

There it was. The rebuke Alanna knew would be coming their way. But what else would he do? Joe took her arm again and pulled her to his side.

"We've done exactly what we were assigned to do. At least the first step," he almost growled at Morgan. Alanna wanted Joe to shut up and not pour grease on the fire.

"And I have some information for you. For your next step," Morgan answered.

"Do you know where her son is?" Alanna pulled away from Joe again. It was not easy. A part of her, the part that ached to be in his arms, caressed and kissed by him, longed to stay as close to him as humanly possible, enveloped in his arms, while the other part, the part of her that knew the only way she would ever move on from Transition was to grant Carla's wish, pushed at her to disengage from Joe, to resist the temptation of his advances. So she took his arm and pushed it to his side, took a step toward Morgan, her choice clear now. It was moving on she wanted. Later, perhaps, she could convince Joe this was his path, too.

"He's not far away. In fact," Morgan's voice lowered, "he's very close by. But you'll have to hurry, because time is running out for you two. If you use The Manifest, it will take you to him." With that Morgan jingled the coins in his cup and approached the next passerby, who stopped briefly to donate some loose change to Morgan's cause.

Chapter Nineteen

It took years for Carla's home to become a refuge, taking in people who needed a place to find their lives again, feeding them and listening to their stories or leaving them alone if they were not ready to face whatever had led them to such despair that they'd almost given up. Where other people saw something to ignore, Carla saw a seed to nurture.

Before Marv moved in there had been old lady Eustace, who talked to herself and wore a hat indoors. Something had happened to her, but Carla never asked and always treated her like anyone else. One day she trudged down the stairs, dragging a small suitcase behind her and said to Carla, "Going to my sister in Far Rockaway now. Thank you for everything. I feel better." At the bottom step she handed Carla a large, padded, manila envelope.

"What's this?" Carla turned it over, but it had no writing on it and was sealed tightly with Scotch tape.

"Open that tomorrow. I'll be with my sister by then. Won't be back."

As she pulled her bag out the door, she smiled once before walking away in the direction of the subway. Carla never saw her again. But she knew old lady Eustace was all right, knew in her heart, the way you know that tomorrow the sun will appear again over the horizon.

Carla laid the envelope on the kitchen table thinking she would open it later, that it was probably some old magazine articles or perhaps newspaper clippings. Why she thought that, she really didn't know. It just seemed like something old lady Eustace would have done in her time alone, up on the third floor. Maybe it would turn out to be stories about how old lady Eustace had gotten there or about her past.

When Carla finally got around to opening the envelope, she nearly fell over. Inside was a thick wad of hundred dollar bills, so thick, in fact, and packed in so tightly that Carla had to cut the envelope to release them. She counted out twenty thousand dollars, setting it in front of her in twenty stacks of one thousand each, and then she just sat there in the kitchen staring at all this money and thinking, where did old lady Eustace get this, and if she had it, why did she stay here so long?

The next day, after she'd had time to think about that money, she took half of it over to the mission for the homeless, because, she thought, everyone needs a home or someplace they can go when they've lost their home. She stored the rest in her dresser. Later, after Marv showed up, after he moved in and restored her house, he built a hidden recess—like a wall safe—in the library room downstairs where Carla could hide things in plain sight.

That's how it was with Raoul. The first time she had met Raoul he had been arrested for fighting in a bar six blocks from the mission. She had gotten a call at two in the morning and run down to the station, a coat thrown over her bathrobe and gown, bail money in her pocket and sleep in her eyes. She was well known at the station. She made frequent appearances on behalf of whoever needed a helping hand. She had taken one look at Raoul's busted-up face and decided on the spot that he was worth rescuing, even though he was still drunk, sitting on the floor of a semilit cell and muttering about some woman named Jasmine.

Carla took him home and nursed his wounds, scolding him and making pot after pot of strong coffee until dawn. Finally he had fallen asleep on the couch. Carla never did find out who

93

Jasmine was, and she felt it was better not to know. She did, however, hear all about Raoul's career in the ring and how he had refused to throw his last fight. Losing the mob's money was not exactly a brilliant career move, and after that he'd had no goals and no one to keep him on the right path.

After learning how to cook everything from Russian borscht to French soufflés, he'd long since taken over running the café . He could make corn pone and grits, stuff a turkey with chestnut puree and baked the best meat loaf in Brooklyn.

While Raoul took over Carla's Home Cooking, Marv became as much a part of Carla's house as the kitchen sink. They became the bookends of Carla's life, one watching after her at work, the other at home. While Marv put his own life back together and refurbished Carla's once elegant but by then shabby house, he noted the comings and goings of others in need. None of them ever seemed a threat to Carla or anyone but themselves until Tempest arrived.

At the same time that Alanna and Joe were sharing their true mission with Carla, Tempest breezed into the house, walking along the path by the side of the house and opening the back kitchen door by the garden instead of the front door, as if she didn't want anyone to see her comings and goings. How she'd gotten a key to that door would later be a question for Marv, one that he would forget to ask Carla and that he would regret, thinking if only he'd been more vigilant he could have changed something about what happened. He would never be sure what he could have done differently, only that he wished he had.

At that moment Marv was awkwardly positioned on his side on the floor fixing a pipe under the sink, Bugs lying nearby half asleep. Before the door even opened, Bugs came to life and a deep rumbly growl emerged from his throat. Marv twisted his neck and tilted his head sideways so he could see Bugs.

"What's got into you?" he asked the dog, not expecting a reply, of course, and Bugs growled again.

Then Marv heard the deadbolt slide, and the door opened and he saw slender legs and black shoes as a woman's feet came into view. He knew who it was. There were only the two of them and Carla living at the house at that time. He wriggled out and sat up, a wrench in one hand, a rag in the other.

"Someone ought to shut that mutt up," Tempest glared at Bugs, then turned to Marv. She smiled sweetly as if she hadn't just insulted his dog. "Well, the master builder fixes plumbing, too. Useful man to have around the house." She bent down, licked her top lip with the tip of her tongue, and peered into Marv's eyes intently. The way she was standing, Marv could clearly see down her blouse to her bra and the tops of her breasts. He blushed a deep, embarrassing red until the tips of his ears felt hot. He thought he should look away but he couldn't. It was like something had locked him into place. The hand holding the wrench felt stiff, and once again Bugs growled softly.

Tempest knelt on the floor with one knee, her black pencil skirt pulling tightly up around her hips, and Marv wondered if she hadn't been cold out there dressed like that in the March wind, but before he could say anything, she reached out and placed the pads of her fingers under his stubbly chin (for Marv hadn't yet shaved and it was after lunchtime by then) and tilted his face up towards her, drawing his eyes away from her breasts.

"Maybe you could fix something up in my room?" she asked. "It wouldn't take long." She moved her head back and forth slightly and smiled, raising her eyebrows. "Maybe tonight? After I get back from work?"

Marv didn't know what to say. Or just couldn't speak at that moment. She released his chin and stood up quickly, pulling her skirt straight around her thighs, wriggling a little to get the wrinkles free—or maybe just to tease Marv. She stood like that in front of him for a few seconds longer than she had to, legs apart, skirt tight against her legs outlining her slender body.

"Leave the dog behind, though. I'm allergic." With that, she walked through the kitchen, and he heard her climb the stairs to the third floor, where Carla had given her the back room facing the garden.

Bugs got up and walked over to Marv and poked his nose at Marv's hand frozen in midair holding the wrench. Marv let the hand relax finally and shook his head.

"Waddya know, old boy, waddya know," he muttered to Bugs. "You don't like her much. I can see that. Now what's a young thing like her making goo goo eyes at an old man like me for? Think I should go on up there one night and find out?" He stroked Bugs behind one ear, and Bugs collapsed next to him.

Chapter Twenty

She was glad to have made a new conquest, even if it was only that old rummy from the second floor. Mr. Fixit, she thought to herself and laughed out loud while she studied herself in the mirror. The bruises were fading but the scratch marks still showed on her arms. He'd been too rough. She told him that in the bar, but he just shrugged it off.

"You gotta make it look real," he said, waving a thick-fingered hand in the air. "Anyways, I'm the one got bashed up good. I should charge you more for that. Hurts like hell. I'd like to go back and bash her like she done me. Waddya say, sugar, we both go over there and rob her till and bash her up good."

Tempest just stared at his hands. She hated those fingers. Stubby, grotesque looking. But useful. When a girl needed them. And of course he had put them in places she didn't like to think about. Places even in her own body. When she'd had to let him. To get him to do something she wanted done. Well, it was over for now. He couldn't touch her anymore. But she still had to carry on with the pretense, so at the bar she'd let him put his hand on her thigh and his nose against her neck. Let him whisper things and giggled at him. She winced, remembering it, but also smiled to herself, that wicked little smile she'd learned so long ago. That rummy downstairs couldn't be worse. And he could be useful, what with the full run of the house. She could use him before it was all over. He knew where things were in this house. Knew all the hiding places. She was sure of it.

The one with the stubby hands wanted more money. It always came down to that. Tempest was tired of such paltry demands when she was after a commodity that was beyond measuring.

In London, money was there automatically because of her law firm partnership. She'd looked older then, and anyway, that was before. This was a new game. She had to get money some other way, and she'd found that looking like a teen had its advantages. For one thing, a woman named Carla wanted to protect her. And a woman like that, who owned so much, a woman like that would have hiding places in this big house, places where she kept valuable things, jewelry perhaps that she didn't think about often and couldn't conceive would ever disappear and wouldn't know for months—years, maybe—that they were gone. And women like that always kept some valuables in the house, never suspecting that a stranger could find any hiding place. She'd known women who had hidden their jewels in the freezer, hidden cash in a flowerpot, kept gold in a baby's humidifier. If it was there, Tempest could find it.

*

At this point for Carla, waiting was like sitting by a stick of dynamite watching the lit fuse sputter and creep ever closer. She tried to keep busy, Raoul monitoring her the way his boxing coach used to hover over him. He didn't know exactly what was going on but he knew it was significant. It's that girl, he kept thinking. The one from the alley. It's stirred something in Carla. She won't tell me straight out. I know her. But there's something with that girl. Can't put my finger on it, but something.

Thoughts like these ran over and over in his mind as he worked in the kitchen, took orders, supervised the staff. Every once in a while he went out back behind the restaurant and just stared at the dumpster, as if it held some secret that, if only he could coax it free, would solve all the puzzles he couldn't put together. Behind all the other thoughts was a vague cloud about those two people—the man and woman—who had come to the restaurant and talked to Carla.

"Why don't you tell me what's going on?" Raoul finally asked Carla. "You jumpy as a rabbit in a lettuce patch."

"I can't tell anyone. If I could I would tell you right off. Maybe soon I can. But not now."

That sealed it and Raoul stopped asking. But he still watched her closely as she wrung her hands, drummed her fingers, and sighed like she could never get enough air. Detective Mathews came back just before closing that night. Asked Raoul for a piece of pie and a coffee because Carla seemed too distracted to take an order, and all the wait staff had gone.

"What kind of pie you want?"

"What's best?"

"Depends on your taste buds. All my pies are the best you'll ever find."

"Surprise me," Detective Mathews grinned at him and shrugged out of his coat. "What's going on?" He nodded toward Carla sitting alone way at the corner booth. "She okay?"

"You tell me. Won't talk about it. Won't tell me a thing." He plunked a piece of warmed apple pie on the counter and filled a mug with coffee. Then he disappeared and reappeared with a dish of what looked like vanilla ice cream. "On the house," he said. "Make the ice cream right here myself. It's walnut. Goes good with that pie."

"Thanks." Detective Mathews slipped the silverware into his jacket pocket along with a napkin, scooped the ice cream onto the pie and picked up the mug and plate and walked over to where Carla had stationed herself. He slid in across from her.

"Hello, beautiful," he said softly. Carla looked up, startled to see him and also, in a strange way that she hadn't yet begun to think about, relieved to see him.

"Who you calling beautiful?"

"You. Do you mind?"

"I don't know. I'll have to consider it."

"What's there to consider?"

"What you're after. Seems to me like you work some mighty odd hours."

"Same hours you work." And he repeated it. "Beautiful."

"Watch yourself. You getting mighty familiar, Detective Mathews."

Detective Mathews ate his pie and ice cream. It was just as good as Raoul said it would be. He picked up the mug and drank some coffee, all the while studying Carla. And thinking. What was it about her that attracted him? Well, you never could tell about that sort of thing. I must want to settle down with a good woman, he thought. Must be something about her that reminds me of home. That was it. She felt like home when he was around her. He looked around and realized even the restaurant had a comfortable feeling about it. Something in the atmosphere, even though it was a business. It was also a personal reflection of her and, he thought, it is beautiful.

"Call me Lou, Carla. I think we're about to move into a new phase."

Carla's eyes widened. She tilted her head to the side and placed her hands on the table as if to push herself out of the booth, but then she didn't move, and Lou Mathews took that as a good sign and placed his left hand, the one not holding the coffee mug, on top of hers and squeezed it a little.

"That's right, beautiful," he said in that caramel voice of his, "a new and more personal phase. That's okay with you, isn't it?"

Chapter Twenty-One

"Damn, Morgan," Joe muttered under his breath as he watched Morgan disappear like an apparition down the street, jingling his cup and change. He turned to Alanna and tried to encircle her waist again, to get back to where they'd been, but Alanna was having none of it now.

"What did he mean by time was running out for us? I'm scared, Joe. What's going to happen?"

"What's going to happen is, we're going back to the B & B and continue what we started." He pulled her close and nuzzled her neck, but she turned her head to stare into his eyes.

"We have to use The Manifest to find Carla's son now, so behave yourself." She disengaged from his arms and looked around for a good place to dematerialize. Joe frowned. Standing on the sidewalk, his plans thwarted, he looked like a sullen teenager.

"Come on," Alanna motioned to him. "We'd better hurry. I don't want to find out what might happen if we run out of time." What could they do to us, she wondered. After all, they were as close to dead as anyone could get. Then again, to right that wrong was her goal and she didn't want anything standing in the way of that. Joe was another story altogether. He wanted to move on. He still wanted the perks of life on Earth. Perks like her. Men . . . she thought. Always a one-track mind.

Joe followed as she hurried to slip behind a construction fence that had a board missing. It was a site where some building had been demolished but work on whatever was to replace it had not yet begun, so it was empty of people, with a few machines sitting idly on the chewed-up dirt amid piles of rubble.

He stood behind her and whispered, "He's just saying that so we won't get together. Probably jealous that he can't get it for himself anymore."

"Is that what I am to you? Getting some?"

"No, no, but you know what I mean." He slipped through the space behind her, and now they both stood looking around at the vacant lot. "That came out wrong. I'm just pissed. And frustrated. Every time we get close something pulls us apart. I'm pissed about that but also at this lack of control of my own destiny. It sucks."

He looked so pathetic that Alanna softened. She came to his side and took his arm. "Come on. Maybe once we get this wish granted, we can ask for a vacation, for some time to ourselves. Although I'm not sure what time even means anymore. Or how someone in Transition takes a vacation. I mean, where would we go?"

Before she could decide on the best place to engage The Manifest, Joe was kissing her, holding her tightly so she couldn't get away, and this time she didn't resist, only returned his kiss and wrapped her arms around his broad shoulders. She could feel his tight muscles as he bent her slightly back and held her head between his hands. And then, as if some unseen force, determined to keep them apart had heard Joe's complaint, they began to fade, even as their bodies ached to merge.

*

Tempest awoke groggy and a little confused. Day or night, it didn't make any difference to her. She had no idea what time it was or even what day but realized in a foggy sort of way that she did have to get to work. She leaned as far over the bed as she could to reach the window shade and tugged at the corner. Night. It was dark. But how late? She tumbled out of bed, scratching around at the dresser to find the watch she'd stolen a few days ago. It was cheap but worked. She switched on the light. The clock read ten thirty-eight. That left her twenty minutes to get cleaned up and over to the bar for the late shift. She hoped Benny Fingers wouldn't be there. He'd said he was getting nervous about hanging around town waiting for the rest of his money. He had a feeling someone was watching him but he wasn't sure who or why. Guys like Benny had an instinct for trouble.

Well, that was his problem, Tempest thought. She had her own concerns. First was to get that rummy to show her the rest of the house. He kept odd hours, so she would have to make a point of listening for his footsteps on the stairs or catching him in the kitchen. Maybe when she was getting back from the bar early in the morning.

She pulled on a short black skirt and black tights, slid her feet into lace-up boots that came up past her knees leaving just the right amount of thigh showing to ensure good tips, wriggled her hands down the sleeves of a red sweater with a scoop neck. Her bruises were fading but still showed on her neck, so she ran a comb through her hair and parted it to the side away from the bruises, letting it hang down in soft curls over one shoulder. A large barrette clipped the other side back behind her ear.

Her face in the mirror over the dresser was pale. A splash of red lipstick and some green eye shadow with a brush of rouge on her cheeks perked up her look. At the last minute, before she opened the door to her room, she fastened a slender silver chain around her neck and let it hang down between her boobs. Let those men in the bar imagine where it ended, she thought and smiled to herself. Men were so dumb. A smart girl could get anything she wanted out of them. She grabbed the jacket she had lifted from a hook on the back of the door at a store on Court Street three nights ago, and with her hand on the doorknob ready to open it and make her way quietly down the stairs and out the door, she stopped to listen.

It was him. She was sure of it. Carla wouldn't be back from closing the restaurant yet. It couldn't be anyone else. And she didn't hear that mangy cur. He was alone. But if she started up with him now, she'd be late. What to do?

She opened the door and almost ran out, determined to arrive at his landing before he did or meet him on the stairs. It was perfect. But his room was on the second floor, so she had to move quickly and make two landings down or she'd miss him. She did it, appearing in a big hurry just as he was midway between the first and second floor, and Tempest made sure to almost bump into him as she ran down the steps.

"Oh," she sounded surprised that anyone else was even in the house, and then she made it even better by falling onto the step by his feet so he had to help her up.

"Are you okay?" Marv's voice had a concerned edge that Tempest knew she could use to her advantage.

"Ow, my ankle," she whined. "I think I twisted it." Damn work, she thought. I can say my landlady stopped to talk to me and I couldn't get away, make up some story about her.

"Here, let me look at it." Marv stooped down next to her on the step but saw she was wearing boots, so he looked into her eyes, which she'd managed to make tear up. This confused

Marv, especially since their last encounter had left him wondering what he would do the next time they met.

"We'll have to get that boot off to look at it," he told her and looked down at her feet again.

"Is it going to hurt?"

"I hope not, but if it does we might have to cut that boot off. I'm sorry. I didn't see you coming."

"Oh, no, it's my fault. I was hurrying to get to work. Maybe you could help me to your room. It's right here isn't it?"

Her voice was sweet and smooth as Marv took her arm and helped her hobble up the last two steps. At the landing he told her to wait while he unlocked his room door, then he led her to a small couch and let her down gently. He pulled over a footstool and rested her leg on it.

"I guess I should call work and tell them I'll be late."

"You're working at this time of night? Isn't that dangerous for a young girl like you?"

Tempest shrugged as Marv unlaced her boot slowly and with great care. "I have to make money somehow. Working at the bar was all I could find."

"Don't you have to be twenty-one to work in a bar?"

"Eighteen in New York. I'm eighteen. Legal for anything."

When Marv looked up, she smiled at him.

"Let's get this boot off and see how the ankle looks."

Tempest knew there was nothing wrong with her ankle, but she winced and made noises as Marv gently released her foot from the boot and slid it off, slowly revealing her calf and ankle.

"I'm afraid to touch it. Can you feel around to be sure it's okay?"

Tempest knew exactly what she was doing. And poor Marv had no clue. He ran his hand slowly down her calf, kneading the muscle a bit as he went until he reached the ankle. He placed

106

his fingertips on either side and squeezed very gently. Tempest made a show of pulling her leg back a little and saying "Ow," but other than that she let his hands caress and prod freely.

"That feels good," she murmured. "Don't stop." She leaned back in the chair so that her legs spread slightly, and she let her other leg stretch out until it brushed against Marv's hip where he knelt on the floor. When he felt her leg against him, he jerked back suddenly and immediately a blush spread up from his neck. When was the last time a pretty woman had paid attention to him? He tried to remember. Vague images of his wife came to him as if from someone else's life. They had been happy once, hopeful, amorous, unable to keep their hands off each other. That was before events overtook them and their lives disintegrated and he spiraled down and down.

"I, uh, I think you're okay. You can get to work and maybe just ice it when you get back here later."

"I'd rather you massage it a little more."

"I don't think that's a good idea."

"Are you afraid? Of me?"

Marv sat back on the floor away from her and looked up into her pretty face with the big dark eyes. A man could swim in those eyes, he thought, at the same time thinking he shouldn't be having such thoughts.

"You were attacked last week," he said softly. "You're probably having some sort of post traumatic reaction. I'm old enough to be your father. You should be interested in boys your own age, going to college frat parties. Not hanging around an old man like me and working nights in a bar."

He pushed himself to his knees as if to stand, but Tempest leaned down so close to his face he could feel her warm breath on his flushed cheek, and he stayed on the floor looking up at her. She took his hand and placed it once again on her ankle.

"At least rub it a few more times. It does feel better when you do that. Then I promise I'll be a good girl and go to work and think about what you've said."

Chapter Twenty-Two

"You didn't answer my question."

Detective Lou Mathews hooked his left arm through Carla's right one as they walked away from Carla's Home Cooking, leaving Raoul standing at the locked door gazing at them on the nearly empty sidewalk. Raoul, usually suspicious of anyone who even talked to Carla, regarded the Mathews arrival as a potentially beneficial omen, but one that would require his careful attention. No way was he going to let some smooth-talking detective sweep Carla off her feet. No telling what that might lead to. On the other hand, maybe Mathews was a good guy. Only thing was, why was he unmarried? Was he some player out to notch his well-worn belt? Yes, he would take some watching. Raoul slid the deadbolt into place and switched off the lights. This was all because of that girl, he thought. She's the one brought this detective Mathews into Carla's life, and now I have to concern myself about both of them.

"I'm no love-stricken teenager, waiting on a man to sweep me off my feet and carry me to some make-believe castle, now, Detective Mathews," Carla told him. But she didn't pull his arm away and he smiled to himself.

"I know that, Miz Carla. I think I know you pretty well."

"Really? Now, what do you think you know about me, Detective?"

"Lou," he corrected her and squeezed her arm against his more tightly. "Well, let's see now. I know you're a good cook. A good businesswoman, that you take care of people who need help. I know you like people. And people like you. In fact, from what I hear, a lot of people in the neighborhood around here love you. And that tells more about a person than almost anything else."

"That so?" Carla glanced over at him. "You think it's easy to know a person just from the outside . . . from what others say?"

"I think I know enough about you, and about how I feel around you, to want to know you better, much better."

"You just a sweet-talking man," Carla sniffed.

"I'd like to take you out someplace special. But as you run a restaurant, maybe something else other than dinner. Maybe a concert. Do you like opera, Carla?"

Carla slowed her pace and Lou Mathews slowed his walk. They were passing by the bar where Tempest worked. As they moved slowly past the picture windows, Carla happened to look in and saw Tempest leaning over a table, pouring from a bottle and smiling at the two men sitting at a table.

"Well, will you looka that," she breathed softly. "I had no idea that girl was working nights. How is it I never figured?"

They stopped walking as they looked into the bar.

"Want to go in?" Detective Mathews asked.

"Lord, no. What would I want to go into that place for?"

"I'm afraid there's a lot you don't know about that girl."

"You mean she's not the sweet innocent she puts on? I know that. A young girl like that—out on her own—some terrible things must have happened in her life to drive her away from home. Probably that home was the terrible thing. I know that girl as well as anyone, Detective Mathews.

Lou Mathews didn't press it. He had a long history with street people and knew that nobody was what they appeared on the surface. Over the years, this knowledge had made him suspicious. Too suspicious, he sometimes thought. Maybe that was what he found attractive about Carla. She was just the

110

opposite. Open and trusting. A good person. A kind person. A person who told the truth and didn't hide behind a mask. A person you could count on no matter what.

Still, as they walked arm in arm toward her house, he sensed she was hiding something. Or protecting something. He would find out what it was eventually, but until then, he wanted to enjoy her company and trust in whatever the future might hold. It was a new feeling for Lou Mathews, hardened by life and disappointed by women.

"What do I have to do to get you to call me by my given name?" he smiled at her sideways although she couldn't see it on the dark street, just heard the smile in his voice.

"Well, now," Carla smiled, too. "You sound like you trying to sell me a car, Lou."

Lou Mathews laughed. "I'm out of practice squiring a lady home, I guess."

"You're doing all right," Carla said. "Well, here we are. Number three twenty-two. Maybe you'd like to come in for a few minutes."

They stood at the bottom of the stoop, looking up at the tall, first-floor windows. There was a light on behind the front door and one outside at the top of the steps. The night had a chill, forewarning storm perhaps, and Carla hugged her light coat to her body thinking she would have to dress warmly if it stayed like this. She turned to Lou Mathews, who was watching her closely.

"I think I'll save that for our second date," he smiled and leaned in to kiss her. Carla did not turn away, which surprised her, for she hadn't thought about him doing something like that and she had no defenses prepared. He leaned in closer and whispered, "Sleep well, Carla. I'll be seeing you very soon." His lips brushed her cheek and stayed there for a few seconds so that his warmth transferred to her skin.

Chapter Twenty-Three

They materialized at almost the same time in front of a house not far from where they had engaged The Manifest. It always took a few moments after emerging through The Manifest to get their bearings and come fully back to life—or not-really-life in their case. Alanna was the first to feel normal. She watched as Joe came into focus. They had been dropped behind a slightly open gate into an alley that led to a church courtyard so no one on the street would have seen them appear. Alanna breathed deeply for a few seconds until her head cleared.

"Where are we?" Joe asked her.

"Not sure. Seems like Brooklyn still."

"What makes you think so?"

Alanna shrugged. "It just looks the same. The buildings, the streets, the trees, the climate. Mid-March, it seems to me. Is it possible her son's nearby where Carla's been living all this time?"

"I wonder how Carla got to Brooklyn anyway," Joe brushed off his jacket as if The Manifest had left him dusty. "I get the feeling she wasn't born here. I wonder what her story is exactly."

"That's not our mission. We just have to find her son and reunite them somehow."

"Hey, I get it. I thought it might help if we knew more about Carla. What if we find him and he's not interested in meeting his mother? Then what do we do?"

It was usually Alanna thinking ahead to problems they might encounter, not Joe. Maybe he was getting used to this kind of life, he thought. Maybe this was what he was meant to do after all. He pulled at the old iron gate and it creaked open enough for them to walk out onto the sidewalk.

"I'm hungry. The Manifest always does that to me. Hungry and thirsty. What I wouldn't do for a not-drink right about now."

They wandered down the block until they came to a cross street that looked busy with people bustling in and out of shops and restaurants.

"Look," Alanna pointed to a sign. "See, fruit smoothies. That sounds good. Let's stop in there."

The place was small, with a counter on one side and a line of brightly colored tall seats against an eating—or rather, drinking—counter on the opposite side. There were two seats open next to the last seat by the back. Above the ordering counter, plastered all over the wall from sink to ceiling, were boards listing the varieties of smoothies available. Music played louder than necessary—reggae, as if the owner wanted patrons to feel they were in the islands rather than on a busy commercial street in the middle of Brooklyn.

Alanna ordered a Sunrise Sunset. Joe made his a Paradise Point, and they carried their glasses to empty chairs by the back wall next to a man wearing a bulky jacket, the collar turned up to meet the brim of a hat that covered his face and neck.

"Good," said Joe. "Maybe doesn't stack up to a not-drink, but good."

He turned to Alanna as he sipped his drink, but before she could answer, the man with the hat and turned-up collar reached a hand holding a small vial across to Joe.

"Try a little of this," he said, and Joe and Alanna both whirled around to see Morgan smiling at them from under the brim of his hat. "Always seems to perk you up a bit." He poured the contents into Joe's drink until the last drop plopped down.

114

Then he put his hand back in his pocket and reached out again with another vial and emptied it into Alanna's smoothie.

"Drink up and I'll show you some more about your assignment, Carla Patterson," he said in that smooth, gravelly voice.

"Morgan," Alanna broke in, "you do show up at the oddest places and times." As she sipped her smoothie, which was now a true not-drink, she felt that familiar wash of energy mixed with—what was it after all, that feeling she had every time she downed a not-drink—confidence. That was it. And Joe felt it, too. She could see it in the way his shoulders squared and his head tilted up, as if he was ready to conquer the world. And then something happened and it was as if they weren't at a smoothie bar anymore but somewhere floating above the crowd, far from Brooklyn, looking down at the city. It was another time and Brooklyn looked quite different, not as prosperous or cosmopolitan. The people on the sidewalks wore clothes from thirty years ago and the cars looked older. There was no Starbucks or smoothie bars but coffee shops and hamburger joints, and they looked rather seedy to Joe and Alanna, who were neither with the people on the streets nor visible to them, it seemed.

"There she is," Morgan's voice broke through the cloud-like softness of wherever they were. "Down there."

Morgan pointed to a girl of fourteen walking purposefully down the street toward a big house with tall windows. Somehow Alanna and Joe could see the outside of the house and the inside, all at the same time. It was like looking at a computer-generated image, and they wandered up the wide steps to the front door, and it swung open for them to pass through like ghosts, and once inside, they were everywhere at once, seeing the

115

whole of the house and its garden as if it were a part of memory, a three-dimensional image of time and place.

The girl climbed the steps, too for she was part of the image, holding a bag of groceries that looked too heavy for a young girl. Yet she carried it confidently and entered the house without hindrance or hesitation.

"That's her house," Alanna pointed down. "The one she lives in now."

"Yes," Morgan said slowly. "But down there, what you're seeing, at that time it was not her house. She lived here."

The scene changed to a small row house, very different from the grand three-story house where they'd seen Carla as a girl. And then there she was again, coming out of the small two-story row house in need of paint and flanked by similar houses in what was obviously a neighborhood in some neglect but not totally gone to ruin. Poor but not impoverished.

"Why are you showing us these images? Just lead us to her son and we can take it from there."

"Ah, Joe. Always the bottom line with you. And, as usual, a little impatient. You may need this information soon enough when you have to show Carla where to find her son. She's going to want to know how it happened that he's only twenty blocks away, and I predict it will be a shock for both of them. In order to grant her wish, well, I'm just greasing the wheels a little bit for you."

Chapter Twenty-Four

"Come on over here, kitties," Carla called and tapped the stainless-steel bowl full of scraps. They came running, jumping, scurrying from their hiding places in the alley. Carla made a point not to look past the dumpster where the police tapes had been taken down and the trash truck was now allowed in. She laid the bowl on the ground below the back doorstep and stood up to feel, rather than see, Raoul at her side.

"Them cats is overfed, you ask me," he snorted.

Carla smiled and turned to look at him. "You feed them as much as I do," she laughed.

"I know it," he said. "That's how I know they overfed." He chuckled.

They stood there watching the cats gobble down the food.

"I think that orange tabby's a new one," Carla pointed to it.

"Could be." Raoul waited. He knew Carla had something on her mind.

"Well," she began hesitantly, which was uncharacteristic of Carla, who usually spoke her mind straight out. "What do you think of him?"

Raoul bent over and picked up the empty bowl. "Them cats eat faster every day. I got some more scraps back in the kitchen. Gotta give them more to chew on."

He stood up and turned to go back into the restaurant, then leaned back toward Carla. "He seem like a nice guy. What you think of him's more important."

He tapped the bottom of the bowl with his fingers as if he was beating time on a drum. "Never understood why anyone would want to be a cop, though. Streets is dangerous enough without wearing a target on your back."

Carla followed him into the kitchen. It smelled like fresh-baked muffins and coffee. Out front, the morning waitresses had set the tables and unlocked the door. Soon Carla's Home Cooking would be full, and Raoul would be too busy cooking up orders to talk.

"What does he want with me, is what I wonder. Forty-three-year-old woman never been married, and him ripe for the picking by some gorgeous young thing. No wife, no children, out at all hours chasing criminals. What is it he wants from me?"

Raoul put the bowl down and slowly turned to Carla. He was going to tell her to let the future happen on its own, to allow someone into her life, to open herself up. He was about to say that she deserved happiness as much as anyone and that this man may not be what she imagined he was, that maybe he was looking for an anchor finally, not one to weigh him down but to tie him to something that would give his life meaning and connection. But as Raoul opened his mouth to say these things, for he was a thoughtful man who knew that Carla was his sister in spirit, he happened to look through the kitchen window.

"Look to me like you can ask him yourself." He nodded to the front window, where outside on the street, Detective Mathews was gazing into the restaurant.

*

"How do you like having breakfast together?"
"Eat your eggs and have some more coffee."
118

Carla refilled his mug and set the pot back on its burner. She tried to sound gruff, but the detective in him knew she was pleased he'd come in for breakfast.

"Yes, ma'am." He ate the last forkful and sipped at his coffee. "Come sit with me. Or do you have a policy against consorting with customers?"

"I got all kinds of policies."

"I'd like to know what they are. I mean, besides the ones I can see for myself."

"You're real nosy, you know that?"

"I make a living being nosy, Carla, and I'm very good at it. Let's make a deal, you and me. I'll answer your questions if you'll answer mine. One each until we run out. How about it?"

Carla tapped her fingernail on the counter while she looked at him sideways. "What in the world do you want from me? Answer me that first."

He put down the coffee mug and took her hand in his very gently. "I'm forty-five years old. I've kicked around a lot and seen a lot of things most people never see in a lifetime. I've tried not to get hard, but the things I've seen people do . . . sometimes I just want to walk away. But where? Once those things are inside you there's nowhere far enough to walk. There've been women. But the women who wanted me were never the women I wanted. And the ones who I might have wanted never would have been able to withstand the life I led. Now I'm not on vice anymore, and even though I have to see violence or at least deal with it in my cases, at least I'm not right in the middle of it."

He turned her hand palm up and lifted it to his lips. He kissed her palm softly, and she could once again feel the warmth of his body through that kiss. She let him hold her hand and it felt good in a way she'd never let herself imagine a man's touch could feel.

"Does that answer your question?"

He opened his hand slowly so she could withdraw hers if she wished but she lingered there.

"When a woman opens her heart and a man takes a little piece of it away with him when he leaves, she can never get that piece back," Carla said quietly with a note of resignation in her voice, almost as if she was reminding herself of a fact she'd learned long ago.

"And what if he doesn't leave? What if he opens his heart and you both find your hearts beating to the same rhythm?"

"Is that the question you wanted to ask me?"

"It's a start."

"I don't know how to answer that, since I never thought it would be something I'd have to consider. But if I had to answer it, I suppose I'd say it was not likely to happen to me. You told me how it is you stayed solitary, so maybe I'll have to tell you why I never joined hands with a man."

She wasn't ready to do that yet, and maybe she never would be able to open her heart in the way he meant. She had never really confronted her past, not the men who'd raped her, not the parents who'd given her baby away, not the aunt who'd taken her in. They were all dead and gone long ago, and now, with one simple wish, she was about to come face-to-face with the past that she'd hidden away for most of her life.

Chapter Twenty-Five

"Well, here it is. You're the man of action. Now what?"

Alanna and Joe stood across the street looking at the house as if they almost expected some sort of sign. Maybe the door would burst open, or a bolt of lightning would strike the walk, searing a path for them to cross. But nothing happened.

It was a tidy three-story house with one of those ground floors that led to a back garden situated on a well-tended block with trees and front porches and a neighborhood feel to it. The houses were more modest than the ones in Carla's neighborhood but still had a familiar look and feel that would have reminded Carla of the neighborhood and the house where she'd been raised by her aunt. These houses looked more prosperous. They'd been refurbished, painted, spruced up, even added onto in some cases. It was a different era in Brooklyn. Things had changed for the better.

A small scattering of leaves were piled around parked cars and up against curbs, but the steps and walkways to the houses had been blown or raked. Some boys were throwing a ball around in a pick-up game that resembled baseball without the bases. The sounds of small children came from a playground at the end of the block, where someone had raked the leftover leaves from winter into piles so that the climbing gym and slide was clear. A few children had divided up into teams and pushed the sandbox contents into a high mound, which they were using as a small shield in a mock firefight with much squealing and the razzing sound effects of pretend guns. The afternoon sun shone low in the sky and a brisk breeze blew through the bare branches. Carla's son, Moses, lived here. Everything about this street said family.

"Maybe we'd be better off trying to make contact where he works," Joe suggested. "I don't see us knocking on the front door. Anyway, he wouldn't be home now. He'd be at work still."

"We need more information about him," Alanna said. "I wonder if we could use The Manifest to see from above without Morgan helping us."

"How would we start?"

"Maybe just go somewhere private and imagine we're floating above the world and picture what we want to see."

"That sounds kinda iffy to me," Joe shook his head. "We'd be better off imagining Morgan showing up."

At that moment a man wearing a slouched hat and a jacket zipped up to his chin rode down the street on a bike with a flat rack behind the seat. Strapped to the rack was a cloth tote full of groceries, with French bread sticking up over the top of the bag. The man was humming, but because he was looking down at the pavement, they couldn't see his face until he was directly abreast of them.

"Morgan!" Alanna shouted.

It came out too loud, and she clapped her hand over her mouth like a child might. Joe just laughed and took her by the arm to reach Morgan before he rode past, which, of course, he had no intention of doing.

"I was on my way to make myself a French dinner when I heard your call." He grinned at them and stopped the bike with his right foot. He pointed back to the bread. "There's a real French bakery four blocks over. You can smell the bread all the way down the street. I think that's the one thing I miss most about being really alive," he said.

"Food?" asked Joe.

122

Morgan sighed. "Joe, my friend, you are so literal. One misses the sensations of scent, touch, taste, feel, the colors of fall, and the blossoms of spring. The snap of a crisp, cold, winter day and the muffled sound of earth covered in snow."

"But you can experience all that in your . . ." Alanna almost said "life" but then realized that none of them were really alive anymore and there was indeed a flatness to this almost-life.

"And that's why I want to get back," Joe told her. "Do you see it now? Can't you just consider trying to come back with me?"

Before she had a chance to answer him, Morgan got off his bike and leaned it against a signpost. "Come over here." He motioned them to the entrance of a small church. "It's empty right now. A perfect place to view the past."

Inside it was dim and silent. Morgan led them to an apse behind the altar. Alanna felt weird going back there, and because the church was so empty, the surrounding quiet seemed otherworldly. She wondered if this was real at all or if Morgan had managed somehow to manufacture some sort of stage set with atmosphere designed to evoke a feeling of awe. As she wondered, Joe took her hand and held it lightly, and then they seemed to float away as if on a cloud.

When they looked down, the city was spread out in an interlocking grid of streets and buildings, like looking at a three-dimensional map of Earth as viewed from a satellite, only this seemed to be in real time, with cars and buses moving, people walking, horns blaring, trucks shifting gears. It was a map, and it was also a movie, the actors regular people but wearing clothes and cars from twenty years ago or more.

There was Carla's house, back in the distant past, long before it was hers. As they watched, she opened the front door to leave, and she was again a teenager, but older this time,

123

maybe seventeen, and she looked sad. They could also see the transitions the house had gone through over the years, as if they were looking backward and forward at the same time. At that time, the three-story house with a wide front porch and a small front yard was meant for only one family. Later, a small ground-floor apartment, essentially one large room and a bathroom, had been added onto the back of the house for what was called in those days "a servant," who lived in and cared for anything and everything. They could see that was Carla's room then, for all her clothes and personal effects were there.

Later still, the small ground-floor apartment's flat roof served as a back porch for a second-floor apartment that had been added. It ran the width of the house but only half the depth. A small hallway connected it to the stairs, which also led to the other second-floor apartment—the one facing the street. On the top floor, another larger apartment ran the full length and width of the house. In total, the house numbered four individual living units, all of them carved out of the original prewar home with elegant, high ceilings and a grand indoor staircase running along its east side. A main room on the first floor had a large fireplace, still working, and three huge windows that faced the street. There was a generous kitchen, a dining room, and a large back garden. An ancient ginkgo tree towered above the front of the house, its roots engaging with whatever lay beneath the sidewalk and cement stoop. An equally tall maple tree had grown from a seed that landed at the far corner of the back garden. It was now a neighborhood fixture, home to birds and squirrels, and one spring a hawk even took up residence, building a large nest near the top.

"I don't understand," Alanna looked at Morgan and then Joe. "How did Carla get here? That other image we watched—the awful one—I thought she came from somewhere down south."

"She was born in Georgia. But Carla's life has taken many turns. Shall I tell you about Carla? All about her?"

"Will it help us carry out our assignment?"

"Well, Joe, you know what they say. Knowledge is power."

"I want to know about her," said Alanna. "As much as you know. Everything."

"All right," Morgan said. "Perhaps I should start with right now. Because for the first time in her life, Carla is being seriously courted by a man. And she's not backing away from him."

"Who is it?" Joe asked.

"Take a look."

Morgan pointed down from where they were floating, in a sort of vapor now. The vapor wafted around them and then cleared a little so that they could see Detective Mathews leave Carla's Home Cooking and walk toward Doyle's bar, where Tempest was just going to work. It was dark now, and they could also see inside the bar. Instead of going inside, Detective Mathews stationed himself at the corner outside a bookstore that was closed but gave him a good vantage point to watch who went into the bar and who left it. Soon a blonde woman wandered to the door, and in a few moments a heavy-set man joined her.

"Hey," Joe pointed excitedly. "That's . . ."

"I know, Joe. Your partner's wife. And do you know who the man is with her?"

Joe shook his head. It was maddening, this seeing reality but not being a part of it, unable to take action.

"But I've seen that guy before. In the bar with her. I thought they looked too cozy. I told Russell before he married her that she'd be trouble, but he was on fire for her. Poor Russ." And then the image of his partner, Russell, splayed out on a

125

sidewalk, a pool of blood running down the curb and onto the street, came back to him and he clenched his fists.

"Steady, Joe," Morgan said.

"Is this connected to Carla?" Alanna asked. "I mean, why are you showing it to us?"

"I'd like to tell you about Carla now, if you're ready to hear her story. And you can watch as the times of her life pass by below."

Chapter Twenty-Six

So Morgan told them all about her. As he spoke, they watched the scenes of Carla's life play out as if on a wide screen that was no longer below them but out in the air, like a drive-in movie, only there was no screen, and what they were seeing was more like a hologram in space.

At the time her mother and father realized Carla was pregnant, her daddy was seventy-one and her mother was sick. They told her they were too old to raise another child and that she was too young. They wanted a future for Carla, they said. She had to get a good education and make something of her life. There were opportunities for young black girls now that they hadn't had growing up. They wanted more for her than their hard-scrabble life in rural Georgia.

After the baby came she never even saw it, and she was told only that it was a boy and healthy. Afraid for her safety, they sent her north to her aunt Sebelia in Brooklyn. Aunt Sebelia, on her mother's side, was a little younger, had never married or had children. She owned a small building with a grocery store on the street level, lived above the store, and rented out rooms in her house. She would free one of those rooms for Carla. It was all arranged.

So she took Carla in, sent her to a church-run school, where Carla was studious and shy. She kept to herself and went to and from school alone, not participating in any extra activities. One day Aunt Sebelia told Carla that she had to work after school to help out. There was an elderly couple who shopped at Aunt Sebelia's store and had her deliver groceries and other necessities to their house, since they rarely left their home. Carla took over their deliveries and was instructed by

Aunt Sebelia to help them with whatever they needed. Putting the food away. Carrying the trash out. Doing some cleaning and laundry. Changing the linens and ironing. Carla already knew how to do some of those things but what she didn't know, the elderly lady, named Mrs. Berg, taught her.

Joe and Alanna watched a fast-forward montage of Carla's life in Brooklyn flash past. They saw her working in the grand old house, saw the elderly couple growing older and more frail, until the images stopped at one point in time—Carla now a young woman but still caring for the elderly couple, wearing black at a funeral, the frail Mr. and Mrs. Berg at her side, a coffin being lowered into the ground. Aunt Sebelia had suffered a sudden stroke and died. The couple leaned against each other, small, slender, white-haired. Carla tottered like an uprooted tree, the world she had come to know once again collapsing. Aunt Sebelia left her property to the church. Mrs. Berg told Carla to come over and move into their house, to the room at the back on the ground floor.

And it was soon after that she heard the story of the Bergs, of the troubles they had seen, about the tattoos on their wrists, of their own losses, and their childhood as orphans from the camps.

Then one day, Mr. Berg had a heart attack. Carla cared for him and helped Mrs. Berg. But he didn't get better, and after he was gone, Mrs. Berg went downhill fast. Carla turned twenty-three, and one month later Mrs. Berg passed in her sleep. Carla went to bring her morning paper and tea and she was just gone.

By then her own parents were ailing and distant. It was as if Carla had never been their child, so Carla thought she'd just better stay in Brooklyn and find a job. She had saved most of the money the Bergs had been paying her all those years. Before she could look for an apartment, a man in a suit came to the house. He told her he was the lawyer and executor of the Bergs' estate. He had to explain what that meant. And then he showed Carla the will they'd left.

It said they left the house to her. And another building they owned over on Flatbush Avenue where Carla's Home Cooking was now located, plus rental units above. One line in the will always struck Carla and she remembered it often: "Because Carla Patterson has taken such good care of us in our lives, and as we have no living kin in the world, we leave our home and our business to her, to do with as she sees fit, and we hope she will show kindness to other souls who may be in need and all alone." It was an odd directive in a will, the lawyer told her, but Carla thought it was beautiful.

In the big old house, Carla had read books and learned about music and art. Mrs. Berg had opened up a world for her. She had learned to cook and organize and keep accounting records. The lawyer helped her set up her business and helped her learn about finding good suppliers and running a business. She decided to open a restaurant, because food brought people together and Carla did not want to be alone ever again.

Chapter Twenty-Seven

"Okay, so now we know her story, how does that get us closer to granting her wish?"

Alanna looked at Joe. He seemed distracted. Morgan was gone again. It was odd how he appeared and disappeared with no warning, but Alanna had gotten used to it, and by now she assumed if they needed him, he'd be there.

"Maybe we should just tell her where her son lives and let her go over there by herself. Let the chips fall."

Joe still didn't say anything. It wasn't like him to have no opinion, so Alanna asked, "What's going on with you?"

"What?"

"Where are you? Certainly not here."

"Oh, sorry. I was just wondering."

"About?"

Joe glanced up and down the street as if he was looking for someone, although who that might be Alanna couldn't imagine. "Hey, want to go get a drink?"

"You mean like a not-drink?"

"I mean a real drink. Like a scotch."

"In the middle of the day?"

"I want to go back to that bar and nose around. I have the strangest feeling that I'll find out . . ."

But he didn't finish the sentence. Just took Alanna by the arm and started walking back toward the bar as if he was on an urgent mission. It was odd, this being in Transition. In real life he went by hunches, sure, but that's all they were. He knew they could be wrong and followed them only if there seemed a reasonable expectation of a successful outcome. In other words, he played the odds. He wasn't a risky gambler, especially in the courtroom with other people's lives at stake. He tried to work out the best deal possible for his client. And he never went out on any limb that looked like it could get sawed off at the trunk. Not Joe. He did his homework and closed most of his cases with no recriminations.

This was different. He'd never felt so strongly that his fate depended on what went down at that bar. Or what was going to go down. He had no idea if something had already happened or was about to happen. But this new imperative to follow a hunch was exhilarating. Rushing headlong into the unknown, with Alanna in tow, well, it felt a lot better than waiting for some sign. All he could think about was punishing whoever was behind Russell's death. That would make all this Transition and Manifest business worthwhile. Except for Alanna. If he did solve his own puzzle and they did grant this wish, would he be able to leave Alanna behind?

The bar was in front of them. He could see the blonde woman—yes, it sure looked like Russell's wife. His widow now, Joe told himself. And boy, did she look dolled up and dripping with jewelry. Russ must have left her a hefty insurance payout, Joe thought.

"Look at her," he almost sneered.

"Who?"

"Blondie. At the side booth."

"Is that?"

"Yeah. And look who she's with."

"He's scary looking."

"Let's go in."

"Joe, if you're looking for trouble, just so you know, I've never seen a real bar fight and I don't think I want to start now. I hear in real bars they don't use breakaway sugar bottles."

Joe shot her a rueful smile. "Me? Fight in the middle of the afternoon? Never happen. Besides, I'm a deal maker, didn't you know? I just want to scope out the scene and see what she's up to. I'm no Philip Marlowe, after all. But my partner did get shot. And I have to get to the bottom of it. It's become a kind of obsession. Like, if I don't figure it out I can't move on."

And maybe that was it, Joe was thinking. Maybe he had to solve this puzzle and then whoever was controlling his not-real-life would release the strings and he could get on with it—either down here or up there or wherever he was supposed to be.

"Just so figuring it out doesn't make you decide to become judge and jury."

"Not to worry, sweetie."

But Alanna was also thinking about her puzzle, and as Joe pushed open the door and led Alanna to the bar, she automatically looked around to see if a ghost from her past might be there, too. You never knew with Morgan just what might happen.

Alanna didn't like the sound of that "sweetie," as if she were some bar pickup and they hadn't been through anything together. There's nothing so rank and depressing as a bar in the daytime, she was thinking. It was dark and quiet, although there were games on numerous TV screens placed on walls at either end of the bar and opposite it. You could watch three different football games at the same time, and if you had laid bets on them, you could drink yourself silly while rooting for your team—or your bet. The place was not crowded. No young singles mingling. No after-work-wine-spritzer types. No girls-night-outs in hovering clutches designed to attract single men.

"What's wrong?" Joe asked her. "You look very far away."

"Oh, I was just wondering what's happened to Bradley."

"Was that his name? The fiancé?"

132

Alanna nodded. For some reason she didn't want to say his name again. Like if she spoke it aloud one more time it would break some kind of time spell. She imagined, in a vague way, that while they had been in Transition, time had stopped for everyone else. But that was a silly fantasy, she knew, like a fairy tale you want to believe when you're a child. She wasn't a child anymore and she knew Bradley would have moved on.

"I thought he walked out on you."

"He did. But we'd had a fight and I never thought it was permanent. He was just going on a business trip and he left mad. That's not really leaving. Nothing was settled."

"Bradley," Joe repeated it. "Sounds very country club. What's his last name. Worthington or something like that?"

Alanna laughed a little. "Almost. It's Covington. Bradley Covington the Fifth. His family calls him Brawley because that's how he pronounced his name as a toddler."

"Cute," Joe said it with a tiny sneer. "I don't think I like him. He sounds like a prick."

"Based on what? His name? Don't be silly. He's a good guy. Just has a lot to live up to and . . ." But Alanna's voice trailed off.

A waitress worked a couple of booths. Alanna could see only her back. She was wearing tall boots and a short skirt—all black, which made it even harder to see her in the dark. A few men sat at the bar here and there, none of them talking, except once in a while to the bartender. They all stared intently at the TV screens. From her perch at the bar, if she turned almost completely around, she could just make out the man with Russell's widow, the woman Joe called Elaine.

"So?" After they ordered a drink from the bartender, she picked up their earlier conversation, wanting to steer away from her own life drama.

133

"See that man sitting with her? He's the same one I saw her with before. He looks like a thug, doesn't he?"

"I wouldn't know. I didn't have a lot of thugs among my acquaintances back in Delray Beach."

"Oh, yeah, I forgot. You were a debutante who lived in a protected bubble all your life. Well, let me tell you that guy is definitely a thug. I just wonder if he's more than that."

"You know, you're beginning to piss me off, Joseph."

Joe turned slowly to face Alanna, a sly smile spread across his face. He leaned over and kissed her on the cheek. "When I was a kid and behaved badly, my mom always called me Joseph. Finally I got a little rise out of you. So I guess even a debutante can get pissed off."

"You are impossible," Alanna told him but she didn't back away and tried hard to hide her own smile.

Joe poked her in the side and said, "I'm going over there and confront her. After I have one more scotch."

He motioned to the bartender for another round. Neither one of them paid any attention to Detective Mathews, who was wearing a raincoat, seated two barstools away from Joe. He'd overheard their conversation while fingering a highball glass.

"Are you trying to drink some courage?" Alanna asked him.

"Listen, I don't need any courage to face her. It's just that she once made a play for me. It was at a party Russ threw for her birthday. She grabbed me in the kitchen and it was all I could do to get away."

"In the kitchen, huh? Is that a euphemism?"

"Ha ha," Joe smirked. "What I'm saying is, she's not going to come right out and tell me what happened. I may have to play along. You understand that, right?"

"Poor old Joe. May have to let some good-looking blonde paw him."

134

Joe motioned for another scotch and put up two fingers for a double.

"Don't you worry. I'll be home early." He downed the drink and stood up, a little wobbly in the knees.

"I think you're losing sight of the reason we're down here. And if you have any more to drink you're going to lose sight of the ground."

"Yeah, I'm just going to go over and tell her I think she put a hit on poor old Russ. Like I'm kidding and hi how are you and what are you doing here in Brooklyn. I'll just hit her with it and see what she does."

He took two steps along the bar toward the back booth and with the third step tripped over something and fell flat onto the floor.

"Whoa. Easy there, big fella." Detective Mathews knelt down and took Joe by the elbow to help him up. "Looks like you're a bit under the weather."

There was something about the guy, some air of authority that Joe instantly sensed, perhaps from his days defending the accused, hanging around police stations, tracking down reports, dealing with crime scenes and courtrooms and juries and witnesses, something about this guy told Joe to back off, not to challenge him, to abandon his plan to confront Elaine in this bar at this moment.

Chapter Twenty-Eight

Detective Mathews became a breakfast regular at Carla's Home Cooking. Showing up at 6:15 before his shift began, he drank coffee black, ate whatever muffin was still oven warm, preferred raspberry jam over all the other choices, and watched how Carla interacted with the customers and staff.

There was something dignified and graceful about her, he thought, and wondered what it would take to get her to go on a real date with him. Maybe into the city, to a Broadway show, or even the opera. Which would be more her style, he mused, dinner and a movie or maybe one of those hokey horse-drawn carriage rides around the park open her heart? He went round and round trying to decide.

This was off radar for Lou Mathews. The women he'd been around didn't expect much and he'd always been glad to provide the minimum. No strings. No entangled emotional scenes. There one night, gone the next. Working undercover let him remain anonymous to the world. And to himself. After he transferred to homicide, when he could no longer hide behind a false street persona, he'd begun to feel like a hollow drum. Everything in his head echoed, thumped with an empty rhythm that had no song.

"Have you ever thought of getting married?" he asked Carla one morning as she poured coffee into his mug. He hadn't meant to blurt it out like that, and this surprised him, because his behavior was always measured out in carefully controlled spoonfuls.

"Huh," she grunted and put the coffeepot back on its burner before turning back to him. She leaned her elbows on the counter opposite him and tilted her head to one side. Today she wore jade earrings that danced when she moved.

"You thinking of squiring me around, detective?"

"I've been considering it," he smiled with his eyes over his coffee mug.

This was too fast, he thought, too abrupt. He might scare her off. He'd gotten good at reading people over the years. He knew when to duck and when to wheedle, when to sit back and when to take control. But this wasn't at all what he'd planned, and it made him feel on edge. There was an unfamiliar queasy feeling in his gut and he didn't know what to make of it. He knew she was holding something back. But what it could be, with everything he'd heard about her and witnessed for himself, he couldn't imagine.

Carla moved away from the counter, putting more distance between herself and the detective. He noted the space and thought he'd made too bold a move. He shouldn't have blurted that out. What was happening to him? He was losing his cool, letting emotion sway his actions. He'd have to be more careful from now on. He had this sinking feeling that he'd squandered his chance, like a tire on his life had suddenly gone flat.

"You don't know me, detective, even though you may think you do," she said quietly. "If you knew me as I really am, maybe you wouldn't be thinking these thoughts you seem to be thinking."

"All I'm asking you for is a chance. That can't be too hard, can it? Just a chance to get to know you as you really are? And by the way, I think who you really are is pretty wonderful. I think you do like me a little. Don't you?"

He grinned at her then, hopefully, ruefully, with a little shrug that said he wasn't actually so sure of himself. That gesture was small but Carla noticed it, took it in the way one takes in a breath of spring air, with a sense that the cold has passed, while Lou Mathews waited to see if the axe would fall. But he couldn't leave it there, not with so much more he wanted to say.

He held up a hand so he could say it before Carla turned him down forever.

"I'm not a saint, Carla, and I don't expect you are either. There's nothing I can imagine you've done in your life that would or could change the way I feel, the way I felt the first time I saw you, the first time I walked in here and saw how you are with people and how you make me feel just being around you. I've lived a solitary life. Solitary, selfish maybe, alone for most of the time, either chasing someone down or trying to evade some disaster. I've made it this far and all of a sudden, for the first time in my adult life, I know what it feels like to want to wake up and know someone needs me—to know someone is there who makes me feel whole. So don't tell me I don't know you, because there's nothing about you I don't know. Nothing important. Nothing worthy of killing the way I feel. Nothing at all."

Carla listened carefully to what he said. She also felt a longing deep inside. But it was confused with the longing she felt from so far back that now she could hardly remember except for the ache she had carried since that day. Now that ache had been touched and brought back to life. How could she look forward when this ache reminded here every minute of every day that someone who should have belonged to her had been taken away and given to someone else?

"We're both too old to be fooling around like teenagers," she said softly, not wanting to hurt him but also not ready to open her heart. "Too old and too used to our own ways. You should find you a nice young thing who'll have babies and make a house full of laughter."

"Who says I want babies? If it happened, I'd welcome it. If movie stars can have babies in their forties, why not you? Anyway that's not what we're talking about here. Laughter, yes. But age has nothing to do with what the heart wants. People fall in love all the time, and time has no clue what age your heart is when it happens. Carla, give yourself . . . give us . . . a chance."

"I can't," she said simply. "I just can't."

Chapter Twenty-Nine

Marv and Bugs came back from their evening walk to find Tempest rooting around in all the kitchen drawers. She was dressed for work in her high black boots and tight-fitting, low-cut black stretch top. Marv couldn't help but take in her short skirt showing so much thigh he wondered where her legs actually ended. He caught himself thinking too much about her thighs, so he cleared his throat to let her know he was standing in the doorway, but she already knew and ignored him, pulling out drawer after drawer. Bugs slithered under the kitchen table. He had no intention of getting underfoot as she slammed one drawer and pulled opened the next until she ran out of drawers and turned to face Marv. She smiled sweetly at him as if she was open to a pleasant chat, even though it was obvious she was annoyed.

"What are you looking for?" It was an awkward question and Marv felt stupid for asking it, at the same time wondering why this young girl always rattled him.

"Buried treasure," Tempest moved closer to him. "Want to search me for it?" She laughed, a low rumbly kind of sound that didn't have a hint of humor in it.

Her black eyes, black as night it seemed to Marv, mesmerized him as he backed up until he was flat against the kitchen door. Bugs let out a loud sigh and thumped his tail a couple of times.

"What's the matter, Bugsy, cat got your daddy's tongue?" She laughed again at her little joke then turned to the cabinets and opened one after the other.

"I bet you know every inch of this house, don't you, Marv?" Her tone was all sweetness again. "I'll bet you know every secret hiding place in here. You worked on it didn't you? The house I mean."

"Yes, I remodeled it." What was she getting at? He tried to follow her logic but couldn't take his eyes off her legs as she stretched as tall as she could on her tiptoes to peer into the top cabinets.

"I've got to go to work now, Marv. Maybe we can talk about the house sometime, huh? I'd love to hear what you did to it. I mean, what it was like before and how you improved it, you know?"

"Sure," he nodded again, wondering where this was going, and again distracted as she put one foot up on a kitchen chair to adjust her boot. She leaned way over so he could see her cleavage very clearly. She knew exactly what she was doing but Marv was a dead man by then.

"Hey, I have an idea. How about you walk me to work and we can talk all about the house. And you can come in and keep me company. Week nights are so slow. I get bored. And not many tips. It's sad, really. Please, Marv. Come along and cheer me up. I get so lonely some nights when there's no one around to talk to." She frowned and looked forlorn, pouting her lip out like a child.

"I don't know." Marv shuffled a little away from the door, but Tempest came over and hooked her arm into his and turned them toward the back door that opened to the path alongside the house leading to the street. She made sure he could feel her breast against his arm.

"Oh, come on. You have nowhere else to go tonight. I know you don't date all that much." This she said just to needle him, because Marv never went out at night and she had made a note of it. "Just for a little while. You don't have to stay long."

Of the many forms intoxication can take, Tempest was one he couldn't resist, and it was the beginning of a downhill slide that, before too long, he would regret with all his heart.

*

"I know that guy tripped me. I just know it."

"Let it alone, Joe," Alanna took his arm as they walked away from the bar. It surprised Alanna that she didn't really mind the chilly night. In her real life—her other life—she would have been shivering and wanting nothing more than to get back to the hot sun of Delray Beach.

"You're getting distracted searching for the answer to what happened to your law partner. And if you don't get back on track, we're both going to be in trouble."

They were walking back to the bed and breakfast, where somehow staying there had all been arranged before they landed back on Earth. Sometimes Alanna wished they could just stay up there—wherever up there was—and not have to grant wishes or exist in this suspension of life. Anyone who wishes they would never get any older is crazy, she was thinking. Not knowing where you stand and what time you're inhabiting was no picnic.

"Why would he want to trip me like that? I almost took a swing at him."

"But then you saw what a big guy he was and thought better of it? Good man," Alanna giggled.

"It wasn't that. I've been in a few bar fights in my day, and I never balked at a guy's size. It's the strategy that wins in a fight, not sheer heft."

"You mean like Butch Cassidy kicking that big galoot in the nuts?"

"Good one," Joe squeezed her arm. "Are you warming up to me or are you just cold?"

She's holding me closer than usual, Joe was thinking. And then his thoughts raced from there to that big bed in his room and the down quilt lying on top of it and how she would look when he lifted it slowly away from her naked body.

The light turned green with Joe lost in this lustful reverie. He stepped off the curb, still hugging Alanna to his side and was just starting to whisper into her ear, hoping she would comply this time, finally, and let him show her how much this not-life could offer them if they could just get together in body if not in spirit, when a motorcycle bore down on them, running the red light with a powerful thrust. Or was it something else? Was the driver aiming at them? It happened so fast, Joe had no time to think. One second they were stepping off the curb, Joe delighting in the prospect of being alone with Alanna, and out of nowhere it seemed, with no warning, the roar of a motorcycle engine was drowning those thoughts which turned, not to terror, but to the kind of shock that befuddles the brain and makes it impossible to coordinate with the body. So Joe stood there, immobilized.

A hand grabbed him by the shoulder and yanked back toward the sidewalk, and only then did Joe come alive with Alanna clinging to him, gasping for breath, crumpled into him.

"What the hell?" Joe yelled at the receding motorcycle, its helmeted rider completely concealed.

For the second time in one night, Joe heard the words, "Whoa. Easy there, big fella."

He looked up to see the man from the bar, wearing a dark raincoat, holding Joe's arm tightly. He helped Joe step back onto the sidewalk.

"Joe, are you okay?" Alanna's hands began to shake.

"Where the hell did he come from? It was like he was aiming for me."

Detective Mathews let go of Joe's arm but didn't take his eyes off Joe's face.

"Hey, who are you anyway and why are you dogging me?"

At this point Detective Mathews did some quick figuring, weighing whether now was the time to show at least some of his cards. Was it too early or just right? You never know for sure, he thought, as the woman took control in a way that pointed Lou Mathews in a definite direction.

"Joe, he just saved your life," Alanna scolded. She had stopped shaking and turned to look down the street where the motorcycle had disappeared. "It was odd," she mused. "The way he came out of nowhere."

"Are you sure it was a man?" asked Detective Mathews.

"I'm not sure of anything. Hey, I appreciate you looking out for me. For us, really. But we have to be on our way now. Thanks again." Joe turned to Alanna, but Detective Mathews once again took Joe's arm, gently this time, more to get his attention than to detain him.

"Listen," his tone had a ring of authority. "I think maybe you need some coffee. There's a nice family place down the next block called Carla's Home Cooking. What say we take a few minutes to have a friendly chat."

He reached into his back pocket and pulled out his wallet. When he flipped it open, his silver badge gleamed under the street light.

144

"Hey, I'm a lawyer. Or I was a lawyer. No, no I still am a lawyer. Anyway, we don't have to go anywhere with you just because you flash a badge. Unless you're arresting us, and then you would have to have cause, which you don't."

"Joe, will you just shut up?" Alanna whispered rather loudly at him. "We'd be glad to have a cup of coffee with you," she said smiling to Detective Mathews. She took Joe by the arm and turned him toward Carla's. "We know that place, too."

Chapter Thirty

Raoul saw the three of them coming before Carla noticed. She was busy totaling up the night's receipts, her head down, engrossed in the papers. But Raoul could hear her muttering under her breath. She did this only when she was preoccupied with some problem and wasn't yet ready to talk about it openly. It was like she wanted to discuss it with herself before she got anyone else's opinion. Besides, she was the kind of person who kept her own counsel, as he'd heard it said.

Now, Raoul was the kind of person who would talk to just about anybody about almost anything, no matter how deep a feeling it evoked in him. But when Carla talked to herself in broken phrases that made no sense, Raoul knew she was in a state. He could read her like a radar screen, every blip a tell. He watched her now as Detective Mathews and Alanna and Joe approached the restaurant.

Them again, he thought. What do they want with her anyhow? She's got enough on her mind. All this started when they first showed up. That's when she began looking troubled. And then that man . . . he only got her in a worse state. Confusing her with his talk. She didn't even feed the kitties the last three days. Now, that means something big is on her mind. That man is only part of the problem, he thought. And then he wondered about the man and woman again.

She never told me what they wanted, Raoul was thinking as he watched the detective pull open the door and walk through. At least Raoul knew what that man wanted. That was one of the things on Carla's mind.

Raoul owed Carla, taken in by her as she had taken in and tended to the needs of so many whose lives were viewed as lost causes. Now she was in some kind of trouble, and Raoul decided he had to stand between her and whatever phantom was haunting her. But just how to do that? He pondered it while he cleaned up the last of the pots and pans and kept a wary eye on the three people now inside the restaurant.

The last waitress still on her shift served coffee to the three people. An empty restaurant is like an unfulfilled dream, waiting for a chance to come alive. Raoul had turned off the music. The ovens were cooling. Dishes were stacked and silverware neatly piled in trays, ready for the breakfast rush.

When Carla looked up from her account book, Detective Mathews threw her a short wave, more to let her know he saw her than to make any deeper contact. She'd gotten used to him stopping by at closing, gotten used to feeling her arm in his as he walked her home, gotten used to the feeling that someone was there to protect her, although she never felt in danger.

Still, one gets used to feeling cared for, a feeling that was unfamiliar for Carla but not unwelcome. It took some getting used to, and she was not yet ready to let him into her life. Walking her home was one thing. Asking him to come into her home was another. He seemed to understand that, which somehow made Carla even more wary. She'd taken care of herself for so long and been so good at it that learning to depend on someone else was going to be a bigger challenge than she'd ever imagined.

He ordered an apple pie and coffee when the waitress came over with her little pad in her hand. It was late and she'd hoped she was done for the night. When she passed Carla's table with the order, Carla told her she would take care of these people.

The girl nodded and handed her the pad while she stripped off her apron, relieved to be done for the night.

Alanna and Joe had stuck to coffee. Joe looked like he was itching for a fight. Alanna perched at the edge of her chair as if ready to leap out of the way should Joe erupt suddenly, or worse yet, if Morgan materialized from nowhere, dressed as a waiter or maybe a bum begging for quarters. He could be around anywhere at any time. What if they revealed too much to this man and Morgan called them back up to account for themselves?

She hoped the officer wouldn't ask them a lot of questions. She'd never been much of a liar in life and knew she would fumble around. Joe, on the other hand . . . she figured him to be good at evading a direct answer. He'd probably get more information out of this detective than the other way around. She wished they would just get to it, but she also knew men liked to circle around a subject, test the situation, mark their territory.

The coffee arrived by way of Raoul, who looked none too happy to see the three of them.

"Detective," he nodded to Mathews and slid his pie over. He didn't say anything to Joe and Alanna, but his attitude said drink up and get going.

When he turned away, Detective Mathews stirred his coffee after adding a touch of cream. He wasn't in a hurry. Finally, he looked directly at Joe.

"I did some checking on you," he said, smiling. "You're quite the mystery man from what I found."

"I don't know what you think you found, Detective, but I do know that whatever it is doesn't begin to cover who I am." Joe lifted his coffee mug, watching for a reaction. "Or where I

148

am," he added, with a slight grin as if he was enjoying teasing this man and had decided to make a game of it.

Under the table, Alanna kicked at him but missed. Now he's done it, she thought. Just what I was worried about. Now he'll have to tell this cop everything. The cop won't believe him, and we'll either be in trouble down here or get hauled back up there to face who knows what. She tried to kick him again and this time landed one on his shin. Joe pulled back in his chair and gave her a quick don't-do-that-again look. As if he knew exactly what he was doing and how it would turn out.

Chapter Thirty-One

It wasn't long after Alanna and Joe had their near run-in with that motorcycle that Tempest arrived at work with her arm still hooked in Marv's. She giggled and strutted and acted as if they were on a date. Marv, whose resistance had been worn away, trotted along beside her with the shadowy feeling that comes when you know you're doing something you have no business doing but feel you're the only one who knows you're doing it. It was a feeling he'd forgotten about for many years—in fact, since his rescue by Carla—but it resurfaced with a rush like cascading water and washed over him, a middle-aged man with a pretty young girl by his side. He suspended questioning the right or wrong of it and just let it happen.

As they pushed through the door, a familiar edgy feeling came over Marv. The dark room, the long bar, the glasses hanging row upon row from a rack, the bottles lined up in front of the big mirror, the secluded corner tables, the TV above the bar, all combined to further numb his senses.

"Sit down over here." Tempest led him to one of the back tables. "I have to clock in with the boss."

She didn't, of course, have to clock in, as she put it. Instead, she told the bartender to start Marv with a beer and two refills and then bring him scotch.

"Give him Chivas," she winked at the bartender. "He's good for it."

She disappeared into the back out of sight and waited until she was pretty sure Marv had begun to drink the first beer. Before she returned to sit down with him, she stopped at the same table Joe had been watching just a little while before, where the blonde woman and Benny Fingers were still seated at a side booth not easily visible to the rest of the room.

"So?" asked Benny. "Where's my money?" He still sported a large bruise on the back of his neck, and a gash at his hairline was partially covered with an old bandage, the tape holding it to his skin peeling at the edges.

"Working on it right now," Tempest smiled and turned to Blondie. "You owe him, too?" She gestured to Benny Fingers.

"She's all paid up as of tonight," he said. "Maybe she'll have another job for me, though." He glanced around the room. "Or maybe we'll just find ourselves a quiet hideaway after you're all paid up and get outta this business."

"Fine with me," Tempest said. "I should have everything I owe you by next week sometime, if everything works out the way I've planned."

"I wouldn't go planning on any romantic rendezvous," Blondie told Benny, which was a mistake, especially in front of a witness. "You're not really my type."

Benny Fingers looked up very slowly, his eyes narrowed and his lips set in a grim line. "Listen, you gotta problem you're gonna need me to solve. And when I solve a problem, I like to know it's not going to end up on the evening news. So you and me, we got a lot in common now and that makes me your type."

"And what if I can solve this little 'problem'"—she made air quotes with her fingers—"by myself? After all, I'm not sure it was him. It's probably just someone who looks like him. It was in the papers and everything. He's dead and gone. Went in a car crash on a bridge. Hit by a truck that went haywire. So I've got no problem anymore."

"You two sort this out on your own," Tempest looked from Benny Fingers to Blondie. "I have to get back to my mark. He should be getting good and wasted by now. Time for me to move in for the kill. And by the way," she looked directly at Benny, "if I ever hire you again, don't be so rough and don't even think about getting off on it. It's just a scam. Remember that."

"Broads," Benny Fingers muttered, thinking it wasn't his usual job and he'd never ever take on one like that again. "Always gotta bitch about something."

*

Marv didn't realize she actually wasn't supposed to work that night, and by the time she returned to the table with a glass of white wine, just to keep Marv company she told him, he was past considering anyone's motives, including his own.

"I shouldn't have this beer," he said. "I'm on the wagon. Been clean for eight years now. Ever since I met Carla. She's a wonderful lady," he mused as he upended the glass and drained it.

"Bet you miss it," Tempest said and patted his hand, letting her fingers linger longer than necessary. "Bet you miss a lot of things."

"Why are you treating me so nice?" Marv asked as the bartender brought a second beer and took the empty glass away. He didn't even notice. He was gazing at her silky white skin and those big, dark, doleful eyes that made a man want to . . . But no, he couldn't think that way. She was just a kid. A lonely, frail girl with no one to look after her. And with these thoughts Marv managed to convince himself that he was doing her a favor by going out with her. That he was stepping in as an older brother or an uncle might.

152

Tempest smiled. It was a mixed smile. Half Mona Lisa enigmatic, the other half seductress mixed with just the faintest hint of innocence.

"I like you, Marv. I think you have a lot to offer."

This was true. At least he had begun to believe he did have something to offer. That, too, was thanks to Carla. He had plenty of work now. People respected his opinion. He was involved in the community, restoring houses, making plenty of money, but still poor Marv couldn't sort through the mix of feelings going on in his head, and the beer had kicked an old hunger into high gear. When the first glass of scotch appeared, he was too far gone to resist it.

"Tell me about Carla," Tempest slid her hand away from his but leaned forward so he could smell her perfume. "How did you first meet her?"

"Ha," Marv grunted. "It's a sad story and you don't really want to hear it, I'm sure. Let's just leave it at that she rescued me from myself and now my life is . . ." he stumbled over his own thoughts, or maybe the beers and the scotch had started to coalesce. "Come to think of it, I'm kind of mortgaged to her at this point. Even if I wanted to leave, I couldn't bring myself to do it. Maybe I still need her to stabilize my life. Or maybe I owe her so much I'll never be able to repay her."

He polished off the rest of the glass of scotch. "This is sure some smooth scotch," he said. "But I really shouldn't have any more. I should get back. I have to get up early tomorrow for a job over in Cobble Hill. These people—really nice folks—hired me to renovate their third floor for a nursery and playroom."

Tempest nodded, as if her only interest was in Marv's welfare. Florence Nightingale working out of a bar.

"Maybe she's using you," she suggested as the bartender slid another glass of Chivas onto the table.

"No. Not Carla. She's like some saint, you know. Everyone loves her. She's helped so many people. Like Raoul at her restaurant. She saved his life, too. No, she's a wonderful person."

"But can't you see the pattern? She seems to search out people who need saving—or at least that's what they are made to believe at the time—and then she never lets them get clear of needing her. I mean, that's not fair to you, really. Is it?"

Marv lifted the full glass of scotch, held it for a few seconds, stared at the amber color and then downed it in one, easy gulp.

Chapter Thirty-Two

Alanna spotted the grizzled face of an elderly man wearing ragged clothing outside the window when they first sat down, but she couldn't say anything to Joe. Not right at that moment.

"So, you say you were a lawyer. What happened?" Detective Mathews pushed his plate away and finished his coffee. "I really shouldn't drink coffee so late at night," he said. "But then again, who knows how late I'll be up, right?" He watched Joe carefully and waited for an answer.

"What are you after, Detective? You know we haven't done anything illegal. What's this about?"

"Well, let's see. I'm a detective, right? So when I come across something that just doesn't add up, it's sort of my job to find out what's going on. So how come a man who's supposed to have died on a bridge in Massachusetts while driving to work at his law office turns up alive in Brooklyn less than a year later? Answer me that one counselor and we can all go home for the night."

So it hasn't been a year, Alanna thought. Maybe Brawley *is* still waiting.

"First of all," Joe leaned toward Mathews, "what makes you think I'm this reborn lawyer?"

"Nice try," Mathews snorted. "Now I know you're a lawyer or you would have either answered my question or lied. I happen to have had a photo of this fellow sent to me. It's right here in my pocket." He tapped the breast pocket of his jacket. "And I happen to know this lawyer didn't have an identical twin brother. So either you're him, or the Massachusetts State Bureau of Investigation has some serious problems in its forensics department. Now, if you've been a party to insurance fraud, I'm sure the state's attorney would be willing to discuss a deal, provided you would clear up the other matter."

At this point Alanna was about to burst. She could plainly see that face outside the window. He was smiling, but there was also something about the look on his face that told Alanna to stop this conversation before it went any further. As she watched, he moved toward the door, pushed it open, and collapsed onto the floor just inside so that his foot caught the door, holding it slightly open and letting a cold draft sweep into the room.

"Oh, look. That poor man." Alanna jumped up and pointed to him.

Joe and Detective Mathews rushed over to the man, who lay sprawled on the floor with his leg twisted back in what looked like an impossible position. Carla appeared, stooping down to help straighten out his leg as he moaned in supposed pain. Raoul appeared from the kitchen, and in the commotion, when Joe got a close look at the man's face, he realized it was Morgan.

By then Alanna had taken hold of Joe's arm and whispered, "Let's get him out of here."

Using the excuse that she thought the poor man had twisted his ankle, and with Carla encouraging them and shushing Detective Mathews out of the way, Alanna rushed him out the door while she announced they would help him to a nearby hospital. She and Joe supported him in such a way that he could hop on his one good foot, and off they hobbled.

*

"What do you know about those two? Especially him."

Carla packed up her account book while she thought about what to answer Detective Mathews. Was he asking as a friend? As a suitor? As a cop? It certainly wasn't clear. Carla had lied only one time in her life, and it had cost her everything. Her family, her home, her life in Georgia. In trying to protect herself from further harm, she had put herself and her family in harm's way.

She had told her mother, when she arrived home near dark all scratched up with her clothes torn, that she had chased a butterfly through the woods and tripped and fallen into a briar patch and gotten scratched and torn before she could get herself out. In truth, she had been attacked, brutally raped, and her attackers had threatened to kill her family if she ever told. So she made up a story.

She regarded Lou Mathews now, standing before her, his face open and honest, expecting the same from her. There was so much she wished she could tell him. So much in her heart that she had held closed off for so long. But she was not sure now was the time or place. Not sure what would be the right time or the right way.

"They seem like nice people." This was true as far as it went.

"And that's all?"

Carla shrugged and hooked her handbag over her shoulder, her account book under her arm.

"Shoot, I forgot my briefcase at home today. I don't know what I was thinking about. I don't like to carry this thing out around like this. Makes me feel kind of naked, you know. Exposed to the world." It was a valiant attempt to change the subject, but Lou Mathews sensed what was going on.

"Here," he held out his hand. "Let me carry it for you. I'll walk you home."

He waved to Raoul, who was almost finished for the night, the kitchen cleaned, everything neatly stacked for the morning rush. Raoul would lock the front door and exit the back after switching off all the lights but the one that stayed on all the time. After what happened in the alley, he had installed a spotlight outside the back door. It was set to come on at dusk and go off at dawn.

Carla handed over the oversized account book, which was thick and heavy.

"Don't you have a bookkeeper who does all this for you?" Lou asked.

Thank goodness, he's changing the subject, Carla was thinking as she answered him.

"I got one but I don't trust her, so I like to do most of it myself. See, that way I know exactly where I stand at the close of a day's business."

"How did you meet them?" He was back to it without skipping a beat.

"Them?" She knew it wasn't going to work, but she tried it anyway.

"Come on, Carla. You and I both know you're evading my questions. I don't know you very well. But I do know you enough to know you're an honest person, and the expression on your face tells me you're hiding something. Now, I also know that you don't know me very well, but you do know I'm not about to let this go. It's not because I want to pester you or get you to reveal anything that's private or shameful or hurtful to you. It's because I care about you and don't want you to get hurt. These two people are . . ." he hesitated.

158

"Are what? They're what, Detective? Dangerous criminals?" She laughed. They were walking arm in arm, and Detective Mathews stopped short and turned to face her, the account book clutched in his left hand, his right holding her arm tightly now.

"I'm telling you they could be. They very well could be. They're mixed up with a very bad situation. The worst kind of situation. And that girl you took in, she's somehow mixed up in it, too. So I'm trying to keep you out of it. Trying to get you to understand that you could be in danger. Do you understand?"

He released the pressure on her arm and they continued toward her house.

"They're not what you think," was all she said. "They're nothing you could imagine. Not in a million years. You'll see. It will all come out all right. You've been a cop so long, you're suspicious of everyone's motives. But people can surprise you." Even when they're not people, she was thinking. Even when they're something like angels here on Earth.

They reached her house and went around to the side to the kitchen door. Carla took out her key and turned to take the book from him. When she touched it, his other hand covered hers and he pulled her close, and before she could think, he leaned down and pressed his lips gently against hers. He swung his other arm around her shoulders and lingered there, tasting her sweetness, and she did not pull away.

What is this now, she was thinking, even though she knew very well what it was. But it was such a new sensation for her, to be kissed by a big, strong man who could be so gently insistent. She let herself be swept in as he dropped the account book onto the stone step and encased her in his arms, his kiss more than a lingering goodnight now, more than a tender gesture, more than the kiss of a casual lover. His hands moved to her face and he held it as he pulled away to stare into her eyes.

"If anything happened to you I would be the most devastated man on this earth. Please, please take me into your heart and confide in me. I only want to protect you."

Carla blinked away tiny pinpricks of tears. Never had she thought she would hear a man say such things to her. With all the people she knew and all the life she'd lived, she'd always assumed this was all there was. This house behind her, the restaurant. Raoul and Marv and the others she had helped over the years. She nodded, in a haze of emotion like a fog had settled around her and lifted her into some foreign world with soft edges and muffled sounds so that they were the only two people in this universe. And when he kissed her again, her legs felt limp and she melted into him as if he had always been there and it was the most natural thing for her to become a part of him. Carla reached up and slipped her arms behind his neck, felt her coat open and her body press against his, felt an urgency she had never before known, and wonderful wonder of all, she felt not a twinge of regret or fear but only a desire for more.

"Carla," he breathed against her cheek as the kiss ended.

He disentangled their arms and stroked her cheek down to her chin. With his finger under the tip of her chin, he raised her face to look up at him. Her eyes were wide open and she was smiling.

"I didn't know," she whispered.

"Know what, sweet?"

"What it was like to feel for someone. To feel this way for someone."

"We have plenty of time," he said. "All the time in the world."

She didn't say anything for a time, and then it occurred to her that maybe she was supposed to invite him in. Maybe she was supposed to open the door for . . .

"I'm leaving you now. I'll see you at breakfast?"

"At the café?" she asked, because she was confused and thought maybe he was teasing her and he was going to come into her house after all. And maybe he planned to follow her upstairs to her bedroom.

"Yes. Like always. Like today. Only it will feel a little different now, I think. Don't you think so, too?"

She bent down to pick up the account book. So he wasn't coming in tonight. She didn't know what to think. This was all new to her. Forty-two years old and such a girl, really. She was embarrassed now, and as a way of hiding her feelings looked down and fumbled with the door lock.

But he wasn't having any of that and turned her around to face him again and brushed his lips against hers hurriedly. "None of that now," he scolded softly. "No need to feel that way. I knew the first minute I saw you that you were the one for me. We have so much to discover. We can take as much time as we need."

With that he took the key from her hand and unlocked the door. When she was just inside, she turned. He stood there smiling at her, a funny, sweet smile.

Chapter Thirty-Three

"Phew, I haven't had to pull one of those in over three hundred years." Morgan brushed himself off and adjusted his ragged sleeves. "And you two . . ." he pointed at Joe and Alanna with two fingers, "have got to get it together. And quick now. The Committee upstairs . . ." he pointed toward the sky and Joe and Alanna looked upward as if they could actually see The Committee sitting in their big chairs at the long table. "Let's just say they have other cases on their docket and they gave me a deadline for you to grant this wish and come back up."

"Whoa." Joe held up a hand. "You never gave us a deadline before. What's the rush? We've seen the son's house. We're just getting a plan together. But I have a few things to work out before . . ."

"Joe, you're not going to be able to work out everything about your previous life this time. Maybe next time. Maybe never. But you have to move on, because if you don't . . . well, things will be decided for you and about you, and you may not like where you end up. It's a warning from them that events have already been set in motion." Morgan pointed up toward the sky again, and his deep gravelly voice had an ominous edge that they'd never heard before.

"That's what I've been telling you, Joe," Alanna took his arm and turned him to face her. "We have to grant this wish before we can do anything about your partner's death or about my fiancé. And then maybe we can settle both our lives and they'll let us decide where we go next. I want to go back. I think you do, too. If only you can let it go for now. We'll settle it all soon, I'm sure. But please drop it now. That detective won't let you go now that he's suspicious of your connection to that woman. And if you keep on like this, you're jeopardizing both our lives—or at least what could be our lives again. Don't you see what a chance you're taking?"

She turned to Morgan to ask him to explain it to Joe, but Morgan had disappeared, and they were alone standing outside the little children's park in Cobble Hill with the climbing gyms and the benches standing mute and silent behind them with no children's voices, no nannies or mothers or fathers or little kids running around. Just the ghostly skeletons of trees lit by street lights.

"Okay. I don't want to make trouble for you because of my obsession. I can decide later where I want to go next." He sighed and they linked arms. "You know what?"

"What?" Alanna leaned against him as they started to walk away from the little park.

"If I could convince you to come back to Earth with me, I think I could accept that as my fate."

"Why, Joe, you sentimental old fool."

"But first we have to get that wish granted. Now how do we arrange for Carla to meet this man and for him to learn her secret? Tell me that, oh, wise woman of the ages."

"How about we give him a gift certificate for a dinner with his whole family at Carla's restaurant?"

Joe thought for a moment. "Nah," he shook his head. "Too out of the blue. I mean, who would it be from?"

"Carla could make it like a promotion."

"Eh. I don't like it. Too gimmicky."

"Okay then, why don't we just walk her over to his house and let her ring the bell and introduce herself."

"You don't think that would have too much shock value?"

"At first it would, yes. But once she got comfortable and told him everything, I think it could work out. I mean, he must have wondered all these years. Wouldn't you?"

"I had a friend when I as a kid. Bobby MacKenna. Really nice kid. Would do anything for you. We once rode a sled down a hill so big it took us five minutes to run the whole thing. Then we had to walk for an hour to get back to the top. He was adopted. He told me during that walk. I asked him if he ever wondered about his birth mom, and he said sometimes he did but that he'd never want to hurt his mom and dad by trying to find her. I wonder if he ever did. I mean. when he grew up."

"Well, that's the thing here. Carla's son is a grown man now. It's not like he could be sent into a tailspin. He's responsible and has a family of his own. And one way or another, it's Carla who's our concern. It's her wish. We didn't make it. She did. We just have to grant it."

"Okay, then, it's settled. We'll take her over there. But what if she balks and won't even knock on the door?"

"We just have to make sure she does, that's all. We just have to convince her this is the best way."

They walked along until they reached the bed and breakfast.

"Well?" Joe looked up at the house.

"Well what?"

"Want to come up for a nightcap?"

"You silly. We're both staying here."

"I know," Joe grinned and squeezed her around the waist. "But we've never had that nightcap. Not yet. Now would be a good night to do it. See, a half moon. Quiet city. Feels like a spring snow's around the corner. A cozy nightcap after a long night on the town."

He leaned down and brushed his lips against hers and as she began to melt against him, they heard the whine of a police siren. It came closer, charging down a nearby street. Joe wrapped his arms around Alanna, not wanting to break this moment. He had waited and hinted and maneuvered and now it was going to happen. He began to lead her to the door, taking the key the owner had given them out of his coat pocket where he had stashed it. But the siren got louder. And in a moment the car was careening down their quiet street. It stopped where they stood, pulled up short, and two cops jumped out.

"Better clear the street," they shouted at Joe and Alanna as another police cruiser's siren sounded.

Joe rushed Alanna to the door and hurried her inside.

"What's going on?" she breathed.

And then they heard shouting and the sounds of a door being kicked in and people running and screaming, and when Joe turned away for a moment to peer out the door to see what was going on, he thought he recognized Morgan among the men being hauled into police cruisers. And when he turned back to tell her, Alanna had evaporated like a cloud. She didn't want to go but couldn't fight the power that took her away from him once again.

Chapter Thirty-Four

Carla didn't know what to think. In fact, she didn't know what to do. She stood in the middle of her kitchen, still wearing her coat, her handbag dangling from her arm, with a feeling of—what? She couldn't quite define it. And what was more perplexing, she didn't want to. She wanted to stand there like a teenage girl remembering the way it felt when he kissed her, like she'd just come home from the prom.

What was this? Not her life. It couldn't be. At her age, to have some wonderful man in love with her for the first time? This was never supposed to be her life. Not after what had happened. And yet . . . people get over the awful things that happen to them. Or at least they move beyond their traumas. They become survivors. They survive and patch themselves up, cover their emotional wounds, and live with the scars.

No, that couldn't be it. Surely it was somehow tied to those wish granters. Maybe they asked you what you wished for but knew something else that you didn't know. Some secret buried deep inside you that they could unearth for you. A wish, if you could call it that. "A longing" was closer. A secret longing that you couldn't even admit to yourself. People had those, she reasoned. People carried around all kinds of secrets, desires, wishes, regrets. Their lives were full of them. Desires that lived outside their scars, beyond the reach of their terrible calamities. Desires that lived within a safe place that no one could touch or destroy.

So that was it. This man, this love, this desire, this possibility, this was all the result of them. The wish granters. If it weren't for them showing up, she thought, none of this would

166

have happened. So none of it was real, in that case. Not Lou Mathews or his attentions, or his smooth talk or his gentle touch. But this feeling she had was real. It had to be.

Standing there, in the dark—because she hadn't switched the lights on after Lou Mathews had turned and walked back to the street—she tried to sort through what was real and what was not. And then she thought, what did it matter anyway. How this man and these possibilities came into her life was none of her concern. Her only wish was to find the son she lost at birth. Her only regret was losing him. The rest was simply a bonus gift.

Before she could move to switch on the light, a commotion and voices in the hall snapped her back to the present moment. But the voices didn't sound familiar. Or did they . . .

"Oh, I can make it up these stairs," a man's voice mumbled as the front door slammed shut.

"Oh, Marv, you just put your arm here on my shoulder and I'll help you up," Tempest said sweetly. She wound her arm around his waist and slid her leg alongside his.

"Come on, now, one step up. That's right."

Marv's foot landed hard on the first step with a thud. "I think my foot froze out there," he said and laughed. "I shouldn't have gone out and had those drinks. I told you I'm not fit to be with if I'm drinking. I shouldn't have done it at all. Oh me, what am I gonna do now? Hey," he slurred, "you have any scotch in your room?" He grinned sideways at her and she knew just what he was thinking.

"You come on up to my room and we'll just see. Huh? You come up and we'll see about a lot of things."

They were halfway up the first flight when Carla emerged from the kitchen. All thoughts of Lou Mathews cleared her mind as she stood with hands on her hips and spoke to their backs.

"What's going on out here?" She looked up at the two of them stumbling on the steps, and when she realized what was wrong—that Marv was drunk—she felt a weight in her chest, and she had to hold onto the stair railing for support.

"Oh, no," she said softly. "Not this."

Marv waved a hand at her loosely, his head wobbly, and it seemed as if he couldn't quite get the words out. Finally he struggled to say, "I'll be all right. I just need to get some sleep. This sweet girl is going to tuck me into my bed and turn out the light. Aren't you, sweet girl?" He swung his head in her general direction and stumbled up one more step. He was now only two steps from the landing.

"I'll take care of him, Ms. Patterson. He'll be okay in the morning. He just got a little ahead of himself tonight."

Now Carla started to get suspicious. "And how did he do that, Missy? Marv hasn't had a drink in many years now. I know because I nursed him through before. I know because I got him into the program. I know because he had nothing when he showed up picking through my dumpster. He is not going back to that. Not while I'm alive to see it never happens."

Tempest, having no answer to that, helped Marv onto the landing and to his room. She led him to his bed and allowed him to slump onto it, shoes still on, and then she leaned down close enough that he could smell her perfume and feel her soft hair on his cheek. He reached up and fondled her breast.

"Such a pretty girl," he mumbled.

"Tell me, Marv," she whispered.

He blinked and moved his hand down to her slender hip. "Tell you what?"

"When you rebuilt Carla's house. Tell me where you put the safe."

"Safe?" his hand slipped from her hip onto the bed.

168

Tempest knew she had to get him talking fast before he passed out. She thought maybe she should run to her room and get the bottle of gin she'd stashed there. But she worried he would be asleep by the time she got back. She had to get it out of him now, so she slid onto the bed next to him and wound her leg around him and slid her body along his side.

He turned to her and leaned in for a kiss. but she pulled back.

"Tell me first," she whispered. "Where is it hidden?"

"No safe," he slurred and tried to reach under her skirt. "No safe in the house."

She let him slide his hand up her thigh. "What then? She has to hide her valuables somewhere."

"Whale of a book." Before his hand went limp and he started to snore, he mumbled, "Inside . . ."

Tempest pulled his hand away from her leg and rolled off the bed.

"You old sot," she sneered while she tried to unravel what he'd said. Was it just the drunken ranting of a man who'd lost it? "You better not remember any of this tomorrow or you're in big trouble."

Before she went to her room, she clattered down the stairs like an excited teen who just couldn't wait to share some great news.

"Ms. Patterson?" she called out, because she had never called her Carla. "You still up?"

Carla pushed open the kitchen door. "I'm still here. What were you thinking taking up with that man?"

"I was at work and he came into the bar and started drinking. I don't know what got into him. I tried to get him to stop, but he wouldn't. He had the money to pay the bar bill, so what could I do? The only thing I could think was walk him home and be sure he got in safe. Did I do wrong?" She managed an angelic, naïve expression, and her voice had a breathy lilt to it, as if she was confused and needed guidance.

Carla studied her for a moment. Perhaps she would have been suspicious if she had that kind of a nature. Or perhaps she would have questioned the girl more if she hadn't been in her own fog of emotion. But the night being more than half over, Carla being in a state of disequilibrium, and Tempest standing in front of her looking like such a lost girl, after a moment of thought, Carla decided that Marv was the grownup in this situation and it really wasn't the responsibility of this little snip of a girl to mind him.

"I guess you did what you thought best. You go on to bed now. You must be tired out."

Tempest smiled to herself, but her thoughts were on Marv's words: *whale of a book.*

Chapter Thirty-Five

"Let's do it now, right now, this morning," Alanna announced as they walked to Carla's café for breakfast.

"You know, we keep eating this normal food—you know, muffins and eggs and coffee—but I have this weird craving for one of those not-drinks."

"Joe, you heard Morgan. We need to get Carla over to meet her son. No more side trips or distractions."

"What if she won't go? What if I need the fortification of a not-drink? What then?"

"We need to drag her out if need be and lead her by the arm over there to his house."

A light snow had begun to fall earlier that morning and had turned to a late winter storm. Flurries enveloped them in a white cloud, and the city sounds were muffled as snow piled up on the streets and sidewalks. People hurried through their morning chores so they could get home as fast as possible. Weather reports were calling for an extended snowfall with accumulation of six or more inches. Already city workers were being called in for duty. There was excitement mixed with anxiety in the city. Alanna had made Joe stop at a shoe store with her to buy some boots. She had talked Joe into doing the same, although he said it was silly and what could happen to him anyway, since he wasn't really alive and couldn't possibly freeze to death.

"You were right about the boots," he told her now, looking down at his feet buried up to the ankle in fresh, white, powdery snow. "This is skiing snow. Maybe after we get through with this wish we can take a little vacation up to Vermont. You do ski, don't you?"

"Water ski," Alanna answered. "I live—er, lived—in Florida, remember?"

"Oh, that's right. You're a beach bum. Well, I'll teach you how to snow ski. You'll love it."

They reached the restaurant and noticed right away how empty it was.

"Must be the storm," Alanna said.

"Good luck for us. She'll have no excuse not to come along."

*

Carla didn't put up any resistance, almost as if she'd been waiting for them to lead her by the hand. That didn't mean she wasn't worried. Because she was. Scared to death, in fact. She came at Joe and Alanna with dozens of reasons why this might be a bad idea. The first was the most difficult for them to argue.

"This is my wish," she told them as they helped her with her coat before she could refuse to go, "but it may not be his. What if he never wanted to know anything about his birth mama?"

"Carla," Joe said in a soft, cajoling voice that Alanna had never heard him use before, "you could what-if yourself right out of seeing your own son with your own eyes. You just have to trust in us and believe that this will turn out to be a good thing for everyone."

"How can you be sure?" she asked as Joe slipped her coat on arm by arm and then over her shoulders while Alanna picked

172

up Carla's purse and handed it to Joe. "People can carry some dark places in their hearts. Maybe he's always hated me for giving him up."

"Maybe he doesn't know anything about his birth," Alanna offered. "Maybe he's been wondering all these years, just like you have."

They ushered her to the door, where she turned to look back at the empty restaurant.

"We haven't had a day like this in . . ." she stopped and thought for a moment, "in I don't know when all. I don't think we've ever been this empty since we opened."

Raoul came around from the kitchen wiping his hands on his apron.

"Where you taking her now?"

"You just watch the place, hear?" Carla called out to him. "We'll be back presently. We're just going over to visit a neighbor for a little bit."

She shook her head and added, "If it don't get any more than this in here, you might as well put that closed sign on the door and go on home before the buses and trains stop running. I never saw a spring storm look this bad."

She peered out at the street, now completely covered in snow, even over the manholes where the heat from all those pipes and whatever was under the pavement kept them warm enough to melt the snow as it fell. But this much snow was too much even for that, and it kept on coming. They could hardly see across the street.

"You got a hat?" Raoul asked. Always watching out for her safety, and bad weather was no exception.

"Oh, go on with you," she teased. "I'm fine. Just fine."

She looked from Joe to Alanna and nodded. "I'm ready."
She squared her shoulders and pushed against the door into the
swirling white and pulled her coat closer around her body.

They walked heads down into the snow from block to
block, and with each block, the snow got thicker beneath their
feet. When Joe stopped at the far end of the block in front of
the school playground, Carla looked up and across the street at
the neat row of houses, now dusted heavily with snow, their
walks obscured, front steps piled high in white powder.

"Which one is it?" she asked. Her hands were cold and her
feet almost numb.

"Down the street. The one with the bike on the front
porch," Joe pointed toward the house.

Indeed, there was one house with a child's bike leaning
against the porch railing. It was a small porch, more of an
expanded stoop at the top of the stairs. Just wide enough to
stomp one's feet and leave a few things outdoors, which few
people in a city would do. The bike looked as if it had been left
there very recently, because it had no snow on it yet and the
wind had picked up. There was also a snow shovel leaning
behind the bike, so someone in the house was prepared for this
surprise storm.

"This close. All these years," Carla spoke the words in a
voice filled with wonder. A cloud of vapor formed in the air as
she did and the snow gathered on her head formed a soft crown.
"Right here. I could have reached out and touched him. But he
didn't grow up here. In this house. Did he?"

Chapter Thirty-Six

Tempest was up early. She waited until Carla left at eight and before she heard Marv or his dog, Bugs, stirring. It was unusual for Marv to sleep late, but after the previous night's drinking, Tempest was sure he'd be in no shape to rise early. And she cared not one bit about Bugs, having successfully neutralized him so that now whenever he saw her, he hid. As it happened, on this chilled morning, when she snuck downstairs with only socks on her feet to muffle any sound, there was Bugs sitting at the back door, waiting for Marv to take him out.

"Crap," she muttered. Then she shot him a withering look and he dropped his head and made a low, pitiful, whining sound. He looked up at the door longingly, since Marv walked him every morning by seven, and he was already an hour late and Bugs was getting impatient.

"Just shut up, you," she whispered.

He stood up expectantly and if he could have spoken would have begged her to let him out. His tail thumped once and then again against the door, and his nose pointed up at the knob.

Tempest padded silently over to the door and with one hand on the knob and the other on the dead bolt, cracked it open a hair. It was then she saw the snow and realized why it felt so cold in the house. She opened the door wide enough for Bugs to get through and pushed him out, then shut the door behind him. She shivered and turned away from it, intent on finding that book. Or was it a book? The mutterings of a drunk about to pass out were hardly reliable.

Maybe it was a cookbook, she thought and started looking all over the kitchen. One thing about Carla, she kept her house neat and orderly. That would make a search easier, Tempest reasoned. Now with Bugs outside doing his business, she had no one to disturb her, so she took her time.

There was a shelf of cookbooks. Some were rather big, so she started there, but no luck. They were just books. Maybe it's a book in her bedroom, she thought and wondered if she should go upstairs to Carla's room next. Carla never locked her door so that wouldn't be a problem. Tempest had been in there before, when Carla had first taken her in. There had been a couple of books by the bed on a small table. Then she remembered the den. That was on the first floor, and she was already there, so she headed in that direction, passing by Carla's small home-office first. She stepped in and looked around but found no books, except those flat accounting books Carla carried back and forth to the café.

She was about to look in the den when there was a scratching at the door, and she heard Bugs yowling to get back in. She would have ignored him, but at the same time, she heard footsteps upstairs. She walked leisurely to the back door and opened it just far enough so Bugs could squeeze in. His coat was coated with snow and his paws had snow caked on them in frozen clumps. He clacked across the room about halfway, stopped and shook vigorously, the snow spraying around the room until the tip of his tail finally swished for the last time and he padded into the hall to meet Marv coming down the stairs.

"Bugsy, what happened to you, boy?"

Bugs nuzzled Marv's hand.

"You're all wet. Where have you been?"

"I took him out but he got all snowy. He was whining to go. I hope that's okay," Tempest came around the corner, smiling sweetly.

176

"Poor Bugs. I'm sorry. Boy. I just had to sleep it off this morning." Marv sighed and sat down on the bottom stair step. Bugs slumped beside him on the floor and rested his head on Marv's feet, as if he knew something had happened. He knows, Marv was thinking. Knows I've fallen and he's trying to help pick me back up. I've got to get to an AA meeting before I screw up any more.

He pictured the hall where Carla had first taken him. It was held at the Unitarian church. But he'd gone to others over the years. It didn't much matter. They were all in the same boat. People fell off the wagon and climbed back on and fell off again and got back up all the time. He was not better than any of them, he told himself, even though he'd been sober all these years.

He looked up to see Tempest studying him. "Why'd you do it?" he asked glumly. "Why'd you take me there?"

Tempest shrugged one shoulder. "Everyone deserves a little fun now and then. I thought it would be fun."

"Was it? Did anything happen?"

"Like what?" she asked, knowing full well what he meant but wanting to taunt him again.

"You know. In the bedroom after. When we got home."

He looked uncomfortable, and Tempest almost laughed but she held it back.

"You were real sweet. A real gentleman, Marv." She thought maybe she could get some more information out of him about the book, so she continued, "We could still get to know each other better."

She came away from where she was leaning against the door jamb and sidled up to him. She stroked his hair and let her hand slide down to the stubble on his chin.

"We're all alone in this big house now. No one would know. And you're not drunk anymore. We could go on up to my room if you'd like that better." She took his hand and rubbed it along her leg.

When she did that, Bugs growled audibly, a long, curling, uncharacteristic growl of warning.

"What's the matter with that dog of yours?" Tempest asked.

The disdain in her voice shifted the atmosphere, and Marv pushed her hand away and stood up.

"I don't think so," he said. "I've got to shower and get dressed. Come on Bugs," he called to the dog and patted his thigh in a signal for Bugs to get up and follow him. They climbed the stairs slowly, for Marv was still feeling a bit wobbly and sick to his stomach. When he reached his room it hit him in a hard wave, and he rushed to the bathroom, where he puked until there was nothing left to rid himself of, and then he lay down on the bed and gave himself up to a fitful sleep.

Chapter Thirty-Seven

It snowed all day, so heavily at times it was hard to make out street lights and signs. It piled up so deep on the pavement that cabs and buses were called out of service. Subways still ran, but getting from the sidewalk down steep, snow-covered steps was treacherous, and few attempted it. The city hunkered down until the storm passed, as it always does, and waited for signs of clearing.

Earlier, in the shoe store, Alanna had said, "Now I remember why I liked living in Florida. Why can't Morgan pull us back up until this clears away?"

"Why can't Morgan do a lot of things," Joe grumbled.

"That's what started our argument," Alanna said softly, as if talking to herself.

"What argument?"

"The one before he left."

"Who? What are you talking about?" Joe stood up and stamped his feet in the new boots then looked over at Alanna. The look on her face told him everything. "Him? Your fiancé? Is that who you're talking about?"

"Yes," Alanna nodded and sat down again. "Bradley. I remembered all of a sudden. Because of the snow. We had an argument about moving to Chicago. It was a big business leap for him. He had major clients there and he needed to be close to them. I remember it all now. He kept trying to convince me that it would be only for a few years, and then he would sell the business and we'd move wherever I wanted."

"So? Sounds reasonable."

Alanna let out a humorless little expulsion of air. "It was not true. None of it. He loved making money more than he

179

loved me. He could have continued to work from where we were, but his ambition was too big. I never wanted more and more money. But he did. He always wanted more. More money. More fancy stuff. More power. More influence. More social status."

She stood up and turned to gather her coat. "And maybe I loved my life more than I loved him. Because I remembered something when we were granting our first wish. Something that happened in my own life."

Joe helped her with her coat and they went to the door, but before he opened it, he asked, "What was it? What happened in your life? You've never really told me too much about it. Only that you were with someone and then you weren't. Was that it? A disagreement about lifestyle?"

Alanna looked out at the snow falling softly beyond the warmth of the shoe store and felt, for the first time since she'd been in Transition, an overwhelming loneliness, as if she were the only soul on the Earth and all its burdens rested on her alone. It was an odd feeling and unlike her. A chill ran up her spine to the back of her neck, and outside, through the wafts of snow, she thought she saw Morgan, walking head down, wearing a mailman's uniform, a gray-blue pack slung over one shoulder, leaning into it for balance. He glanced toward the door where she stood waiting to go out into the storm, and she thought he smiled. It was hard to make it out through the snow-blurred air. But she was pretty sure, and the sense of loneliness lifted. She turned to Joe then.

"I always knew, in my gut, I think, that the trouble between us was something much deeper than all those external issues. And one day I found out I was pregnant. I don't know how it happened, because I was always very careful about that. I couldn't take birth control pills because the hormones did

180

something weird to my body, but we were always careful, you know? Except there were a couple of times that he insisted. You know. That we not use anything. He said it would make us closer. I always thought it would be okay."

"Sure," Joe nodded. He'd always been careful himself, never wanting to get tied down because some chick got herself pregnant. He chided himself silently for remembering the way he'd thought about the women he dated, if you could even call it dating, because he never took them out for long. Never wanted them to get attached. But they all seemed so interchangeable.

Looking back on his past, he was ashamed and kept silent.

"I didn't know what to do," Alanna looked down at her new boots. She hoped they were truly waterproof, because it looked cold out there beyond the store. "But for some reason, I didn't tell him and then one day I was swimming in the ocean and I felt something tug inside me. A soft little tug, and I just knew what it was. I couldn't have been very far along. Three months at the most. I didn't get out of the water. I just took off the bottom of my bikini. There was no one around. I swam close in to the shore because I didn't want to attract any sharks if they were around. And I just floated in the water until the pain stopped and it was all over. Then I put my suit back on and got out and went back home and went to sleep. I always felt, somewhere deep in here, that I willed that baby to abort. That I didn't want to be tied to him by a baby."

Alanna began to cry very quietly. She turned her head away, but Joe knew what was happening. He'd never felt he was very good at comforting a woman, but this time he tried. He hugged her to him and let her rest her head on his shoulder as the tears came down silently and her shoulders heaved as she breathed in with each sob.

"I never cried about it. Never shed one tear. How cold-hearted am I?"

As she uttered these words, the tears came down in a rush, and Joe reached into his pocket for his handkerchief and handed it to her.

"Am I crying for the little life I lost or for myself?" she asked, more to herself than to Joe. "I don't know. I'm pretty awful, I guess."

"Maybe you're crying for both. Anyway, what does it matter? Sometimes things happen that are just out of our control. You could have another baby. I mean, one baby does not replace another one. But you're healthy and you could still have a baby, if you wanted to. Lots of women have miscarriages. It's very common. I'm sure you're just being superstitious about it. You can't lose a baby with thoughts."

"Maybe, but you know, it's just one more possibility gone. Sometimes it seems as if life is a series of them. Of losing the possibility of something wonderful happening. And those possibilities blow away like clouds on a windy day. And what's left is everyday life. Just the same every day. Until now. Until this. There's no way to think that our situation is just ordinary, everyday stuff."

Joe didn't say anything. Alanna held up the teary handkerchief and sniffled a little.

"I guess I'll hold onto this. Thanks, Joe. You can be very sweet, you know?" She leaned over and kissed his cheek.

As she did, he reached up and cupped the back of her head with his hand and moved her face sideways to meet his lips, and this time they did kiss. And the kiss lasted quite some time. And neither of them thought of breaking apart, until someone pushed the door open and a blast of cold air enveloped them. When they broke apart, Alanna saw it was that mailman

182

delivering a stack of letters and a cardboard carton to the store owner. But he wasn't a mailman at all, really.

Chapter Thirty-Eight

C arla's life had all of a sudden spun into a storm of its own. Although Raoul kept a watchful eye on her whenever he could, he was busy running the restaurant day-to-day. Anyway, no matter how he tried, he couldn't get her to let him in past a certain point.

That Lou Mathews, Raoul thought, he seems okay. But I don't know. You can never be too careful. Them cops lead broken-up lives, all the time hanging with riff raff and no-goods. Wouldn't want Carla to have to associate with that. Then again, they don't bring it home with them. But then when they do come home it's in their head, and how they gonna shake it once it's stuck in there? And then he thought, but there's something else. It's not just him. She's got something else going on these days. His thoughts rattled around like that without landing on any conclusion.

Carla had her own tumbling waterfall of thought. What if this, and why not that, and does he really, and suppose I do. No thought lasted very long, and they all jumbled together in a big knot of indecision until she felt exhausted from all the possibilities with no endings.

The snow finally tapered off, and people came out to shovel sidewalks and clear off parked cars. Snow plows worked their way up and down the streets, and a few cabs showed yellow against all the white. And for a while at least, the city was a muffled white blanket of powder.

Carla put on her boots, tied her scarf around her neck, topped her head with a green hat with a bow on the side, slid her arms into her heaviest overcoat, and ventured out. Instead of turning to go to the restaurant, she veered off in the other direction and headed for her son's house. She hadn't been this nervous since the first day she went to work for Mrs. Berg all those years ago. But then she was only thirteen. Just a girl, newly arrived in a strange city, a girl with s secret, shameful past, a girl who had learned from one very terrible day not to trust.

Now here she was, about to take a leap that would require trust in herself, in a son she'd never seen, in whoever else was part of his life. Courage—real courage—shows itself in small ways at intimate times. Carla had wrestled long enough with secrets. The time had come, the world had constructed the circumstances to test her courage. She could turn away from that street and that house and that son of hers. Or . . . she could find the courage within herself to tell the world the truth and take the consequences.

So she opened the door and stepped out onto the ground covered in snow. Her boots crunched as she walked. Not fast, but not with any hesitation. She had no idea what would happen. If he turned away from her, she had no other plan. But she knew that life, from this moment forward, would never be the same—for better or worse. This was her river and she would not step in it again.

Chapter Thirty-Nine

As she rounded the corner and her son's house came into view, Carla also spotted Alanna and Joe walking toward her from the other end of the block. People were out shoveling their sidewalks. Children chucked snowballs back and forth. In the little park there were already snowmen in the works, and snow forts faced each other with boys shouting commands and counter commands while they pelted each other.

Her son's sidewalk, Carla noted, had been neatly shoveled, the front steps cleared, giving safe access to the front porch. Yesterday's bike had been removed. A wide, flat snow shovel leaned against the wall next to the front door.

"There she is," Alanna nodded toward Carla. "I hope she's going to actually do this today."

"That's where we come in. Moral support," said Joe.

Carla stopped across the street from the house and studied it, as if by watching she might receive some message that would tell her what awaited her inside. There was a small sign under the mailbox by the door that read "Freeman" in gold letters. She tried to mentally rehearse what she would say. When Alanna and Joe reached her, Carla's face—lips tight, eyes wide, and the upward tilt of her head—told of a profound conflict going on within her.

"It will be all right," Alanna told her softly, trying to soothe her. "You were meant to have this wish granted. That's why we're here. Everything will work out. We're sure of it."

They weren't sure of anything, Joe was thinking. They weren't even sure if they were alive or dead. Weren't sure what would happen to them next or why Russ was killed or why they

186

had gotten where they were. Yet here was this woman, and they were supposed to help her sort out her wish.

"This is meant to be," Joe told her. "You only have to take the first step and the rest will fall into place the way it's supposed to." He realized he was making a philosophical argument of sorts, but what else could he do? There was no jury to convince, no point of law to make, no case history to back him up. He certainly didn't believe in a preordained fate—at least he hadn't when he was fully alive. So here they were, all flying blind.

"Will you be here when I come out?" she asked both of them.

"We'll be right here," Alanna patted Carla's shoulder, something she never would have done in her own life, not being a physically demonstrative person but rather reserved in what Joe would no doubt call a country-club way.

Carla still did not move. "Maybe I should wait on this a bit. Maybe I shouldn't a come around like this. All of a sudden like, with no warning."

They didn't want to overpromise but had to say something, so Joe spoke up. "Oh, you'll see. He's going to be happy to meet you. After all these years, he's probably wondered many times about his mother and where she is."

"I hope so," said Carla as she gingerly maneuvered one booted foot over the piled snow at the edge of the sidewalk. She stepped onto the street carefully, feeling around for a flat spot where she wouldn't slip. In her mind, she rehearsed what she wanted to say. Or what she thought would be the best way to start, at least.

She would greet whoever answered the door and introduce herself as Carla Patterson and say she understood that Moses Freeman lived here. Then she would say she believed he was a

187

relative of hers and she would like to meet him. She thought that should go fine, and if it didn't, she would have to see what to do when the time came.

She would not say right off that she was the mother of Moses Freeman. She thought that would be too much of a shock. Too confusing, since he had been given the name of his adoptive parents. She was rehearsing this over and over as she walked along the shoveled path to Number Four Fifty-Three, climbed the four steps to the front door, and was about to cross the front porch to ring the doorbell when it opened and two boys burst out, not expecting someone to be standing there, and crashed into Carla, knocking her off balance. She fell to one side, holding her arms out to keep the littler boy from falling too, and they both went down in a heap.

The little boy began yowling. His brother ran to the open door and yelled for his mother. The mother arrived on the porch to see Carla on her back with the little boy struggling to get free from her purse, which had become wrapped around his leg. He was crying but didn't seem to be really hurt.

The mother extricated him from Carla and put out her hand to help Carla to her feet, which was no simple undertaking, since the woman was quite small while Carla was an ample woman by any standards, not fat, but imposing.

"Oh, Lord," Carla huffed as she struggled to regain her footing, holding onto the smaller woman's forearm. "I surely am sorry about this. Is your boy all right?" Carla searched the porch for the two boys. They were over by the railing waiting to see what would happen next. The bigger one was fake punching the little one on the arm. The little one was still snuffling.

"You boys get in the house," the woman said, "right now."

"Look at you," said Carla, straightening her coat and brushing herself down the front with her gloved hands. "You got no coat on out in this cold."

"I don't know how this all happened, but why don't you come in out of the cold," the woman said, although she looked a little hesitant about inviting a stranger into her home.

"Thank you," said Carla. "I don't like to trouble you. I came looking for . . . " but she stopped as they walked in the door.

Chapter Forty

The house had a small entryway crowded with kids' paraphernalia. Skateboards, jackets, a soccer ball, a pair of roller skates, hats, gloves, all hanging on a coat rack or strewn around the floor below. The boys had tossed their coats on the floor, obviously aiming at the rack but not actually hanging them on it. One of the coats dangled half off.

"You boys come back here and clean up this mess," their mother called, but the boys were nowhere around. "Bobby, did you hurt yourself when you fell? I just want to check on him," the woman said to Carla. "If you'll excuse me for a second."

Carla nodded. She was busy taking in the house, peeking around to the living room and the dining room on the other side of the entry hall. Then she spotted it. On the living room mantle above the fireplace. A large group of family photos, framed, standing in a line. She was drawn to it almost unconsciously, for if she had thought about it, she would have stayed where the woman had left her. But she walked across the living room to study the pictures.

There was her boy in his fireman's suit, holding his hat, smiling. There was the entire family, taken when the littlest boy was a baby. And a wedding photo, graduation photos, photos of other people—family members of her son's wife, Carla supposed, or perhaps of the adoptive parents—photos on trips, at schools, at sporting events. The children as they grew, the wife as a young woman in her wedding dress. Carla's heart began to pound. All she had missed. All she longed to have had. All too late now. She wondered, standing there, looking at her son's life, whether she should have come at all, whether it wouldn't have been better to write him a letter and give him the choice of responding or not. That was too late also, unless she simply slipped out the door before the woman came back.

Before she could make a decision, the woman returned, holding her son's hand.

"Say you're sorry to the lady," the woman pushed the boy toward Carla.

"I'm sorry," he said and looked at his shoes. "Can we go outside now, Mama?"

"That's okay, sugar. No one got hurt. You're not hurt, isn't that right?" Carla leaned down to look at his face. She wanted to pick him up and hug him to her. It was all she could do to contain herself.

He looked at her with big, round eyes and suddenly grinned. "We all fell in a pile, didn't we?" And then he added, "What was you doing on our porch?"

"Were. Were doing. Don't be rude, Bobby," the woman said.

"Yes'm," he replied.

"All right, now," his mother said. "You and Willie can go out and play for a little bit."

His brother ran in from where he'd been hiding in the hall. They grabbed their jackets and were out the door before Carla could get a good look at the older boy.

"You have a wonderful family, truly," Carla said. Without waiting for the other woman to ask, as she thought it rude of her not to have introduced herself before, but what with all the commotion, she felt now was the time to make herself known. She took a breath and straightened her coat one final time.

"I know you must be wondering, just like your boy said, what am I doin' here on your porch step. Well, my name is Carla Patterson and I came to call because . . . " Here she stopped not quite knowing how to continue.

The woman watched Carla without saying anything. Her expression said she had no idea what Carla was there for but that she was not in the least worried about Carla and felt comfortable with her. So Carla pulled herself up and took another deep breath and plunged in again.

"I come to call because I wanted to meet with Moses Freeman. I think this is the right house?" She finished, feeling so far she had done just fine even though she had strayed from her rehearsed introduction. What would come next, she had no idea.

"Yes, Moses is my husband," the woman said. "I'm Cecilia Freeman. Those are our boys," she motioned to the front door. "What did you want to see him about? He's at work right now. Maybe I can help you."

Carla had not expected Moses to be out. But of course, it was the morning of a working day. Still she had no plan for that. She twisted her handbag strap, not sure how to proceed.

"Well," she began, "it's kind of hard. What I've got to say. Very hard. I don't quite know where to start. I don't want to be a problem or anything like that."

"Let's go in and sit and you can take off your coat and breathe a bit," Cecilia said. "Would you like some tea or maybe coffee? It's mighty cold out today after that storm passed."

Cecilia took Carla's coat and placed it on the back of a chair. Then she sat on the couch and motioned for Carla to do the same.

"Those pictures," Carla pointed to the mantle, "they all your family?"

"Yes," Cecilia said. "My people and Moses' people and our children. Our wedding. I guess you could say that's pretty much our life up there. Very precious, of course, to us." She smiled at Carla.

192

"Maybe that's a good place to start," Carla said and noticed that Cecilia looked momentarily confused.

Carla told her story, omitting the part about how she became pregnant. Later she would think about that and wonder if someday she might tell her son how it came about. She wondered, too, if she kept the secret for her sake or for her son's sake, or because of her shame, or because of her anger, which in her heart she felt might explode if she were ever to release the safety catch she had closed on it so many years before. In the weeks and months to come, she would ponder this puzzle many times, never coming to a resolution or finding a way to resolve her feelings.

Cecilia listened as if she were a priest receiving a confession. She never once interrupted Carla nor moved in any perceptible way. Internally, in her mind and in her body, waves of emotion, one after the other, spread through her so that she was sure she would jump up at any moment and run from this woman and this room. Yet she sat, like a tree stump in the middle of a field, with the farmer running his tractor up and down, making furrows, turning the earth upside down to allow for planting new life.

Cecilia was a controlled person by nature. She had been brought up in a family of four sisters, the youngest, the most put-upon, and she had developed a way of hiding within herself as a protection against the barbs and bickering, the demands and manipulations of her older sisters, who viewed her as their personal assistant at best and their target at worst. Once she had moved away from home, gotten her first teaching job in junior high, she found being immutable an asset. The class could never tell what she was thinking or might say, and in this way she maintained a certain control and kept them off balance. She was not one of those teachers who became buddies with the kids, yet by the end of the first few months of each year, she had gained their respect, and they actually came to class eager to learn, if only a small amount at times. She taught English. She loved books. She admired the ideas in them. And she taught with a cool passion that transmitted her love of learning without leaving her vulnerable.

"So, you see," Carla was concluding, "I wasn't really sure how to tell him. I'm doing the best that I think for the situation. But you being his wife, if you think he wouldn't want to know about me, then I accept that and would not bother you any more with it."

Although her mind raced with thoughts, Cecilia was quiet for a long while. Carla twisted her handbag strap incessantly. It was unlike her to be so uncomfortable. She realized that. Normally she was the one making others feel comfortable. She realized that, too. She tried to keep her composure, but with every passing moment, it seemed there was even more riding on the outcome of this conversation. Now that she had unburdened herself to Cecilia, she could not go directly to Moses. Now it was in someone else's hands. And Carla had long ago taken control of most of her life. This corner, however, loomed like a gigantic iceberg, always moving toward her, always half hidden beneath everything she did.

Cecilia knew that Moses had been adopted. They had met at church as teens. Then she had gone to college in the city. It had taken him almost as long to become a firefighter as it had taken her to graduate from college. It was a competitive field, and once he became a rookie, they began dating. She went on to get her teaching credentials, so they had to wait a few more years before marrying. But they had been patient. His parents had grown old, having adopted Moses late in their lives. His father died before the wedding, and his mother's death followed before their first son was born. Now Moses had only his wife and children. Moses was now a captain. He was a good father. They were financially stable. Their lives were full. Moses had never spoken about looking for his birth mother or finding out the circumstances of his birth. All this Cecilia told Carla. In the end, she spoke of her husband as a proud man.

"I don't know what to tell you," Cecilia said. "I can't speak for my husband. It's his decision to make. But then he can't make it without you telling him. Perhaps it would be best for you to write him a letter. But now that we've spoken and I've met you, it seems that not telling him would be a sort of cheating on my part. And I would never cheat on Moses. So I suppose we are now, both of us, you and I, in a moral dilemma of some kind. If I do tell him, I risk his feeling What? Cheated? Angry? Misled? Confused? Maybe all those are things one feels when one finds that one's ancestry is a question. I don't know if that's more upsetting because it is recent. But isn't that what our people have always had to face? The uncertainty of who we are and where we came from and how our lives were not ours? I don't want my husband to feel that way. But not to tell him I think would be an even greater wound. Then again," she went on, looking sideways at Carla with an expression that told she was not buying the entire story Carla had presented, "I have a feeling you're not telling the entire truth. Now why is that?"

Carla felt a sudden urge to stand, so she did, dropping her purse and folding her hands one over the other, a gesture she repeated. Tears pricked at her eyes, and she did not want to show this to Cecilia, who, over the course of talking out her thoughts, seemed to have distanced herself from Carla in favor of protecting her husband.

"When does he come home?" Carla asked.

"His shift is over at four today. He'll be home for supper," Cecilia answered. She stood also and handed Carla her purse. "I suppose you'll be back later," she concluded.

"Yes," Carla said. "Shall I come after you finish your supper?"

"Come at eight," Cecilia said. "The children and I have school tomorrow. Can't stay out on account of snow the whole winter." She smiled as she said this and walked Carla to the door. "We'll expect you then. I'll let Moses know someone's coming over, but I won't say anything else about it."

Chapter Forty-One

Tempest had to find that book. There was no getting any more out of Marv now that he had closed her off, and with Benny Fingers impatient to get out of town—he had told her on the sly that he was taking Blondie to Miami as a surprise—time was running out. The only place Tempest hadn't searched was a locked room on the second floor. Carla never let anyone in there, and Tempest had never seen the door open. This seemed like the logical—and only—place where Carla would hide anything valuable.

It was an old house with its original doors and locks. That was one thing Carla had told her with pride. Marv had restored all the original pieces of the house. An old lock should be easy prey with the right tools, and Tempest was sure this lock would yield to her so long as she wasn't discovered and could work at her leisure. The best time would be after Carla and Marv were asleep. And that damned dog. She might have to do something about him.

*

For the past few weeks, Lou Mathews had stationed himself in a nondescript, dark gray Ford parked alternately across the street from Doyle's or Carla's house. Its tinted windows shaded him from view as he watched and waited for something to break loose. But the heavy snow had blocked access to his car, and even if he could have scraped all the snow away, he couldn't move it until the streets had been plowed. That looked like it would be a while. Instead he read through page after page of a transcript he'd been handed just that morning after he'd slogged through deep snow to get to the station house, where a skeleton staff manned phones and went about daily tasks.

Lou Mathews liked bad weather in the city. Whenever the weather went nuts, crime dropped to a trickle and there was an atmosphere of relief at the station. He could feel it this morning. Jokes flew along with a few paper missiles, and when he found the plain envelope on his desk, he was feeling uncharacteristically lighthearted.

He slit open the envelope, and when he got a good look at what was inside, his mood downshifted in an instant. Inside the envelope was proof of what he'd suspected all along. At least partial proof. But all the puzzle pieces didn't yet fit. That goon Benny Fingers, well, this nailed him as a co-conspirator. And he would roll on Blondie in a New York minute when Lou Mathews got him into an interrogation room. The only question now was who fired the shot that killed Russell?

It turned out to have been a good move getting Michael Doyle to place that bug at Benny's favorite table. All he had to do was feign ignorance of the gambling going on in Michael's back room. After all, a few craps, a poker game here and there, who got hurt? Mathews had bigger fish to fry.

Now that he had the proof and could make a case for conspiracy, there was just the troubling detail of where that thin girl fit in. Lou didn't like that she was still living at Carla's house. Didn't trust the situation at all. That's why he'd gone to Carla's Home Cooking every night and walked Carla home. It was purely professional in the beginning. But now . . . now he'd begun to look forward to those walks and being with Carla. Now he wanted more. But his first priority was to protect her. It was a challenge, though, to protect a woman so trusting she brought strangers into her house and let them stay as long as they wanted or needed to.

When he got to the end of the transcript from Doyle's, he saw there was an extra report tacked on with some photocopies of newspaper clippings. And there it was. Right there in headlines with pictures: *Prominent defense attorney dies when truck collides with his BMW, forcing it to plunge two hundred feet over a guardrail to the ground below.*

The pictures showed the crushed BMW and the truck on its side. There was one shot of the lawyer, Joe Taft, looking quite pleased with himself, speaking to the press after he'd won a big case for a businessman who'd been accused of murdering his wife in the middle of a nasty divorce that would have netted her half his business profits for life.

This system, Lou thought, what a mockery. That guy shouldn't have gotten off. Then he caught himself and came back to the present. How this is possible, he thought, can only be because the guy faked his death, because this is the same damned guy. Joe Taft. Sounds like a B-movie stage name, Lou thought. There was a biography on the next page, printed from a police search he'd requested. Joe Taft, only child of Henry and Lucille Taft of Wayland, Massachusetts. There it was in plain letters. This just was not possible.

Lou Mathews was not one of those detectives who had ever called in a psychic to help locate a murder victim or read Tarot cards or whatever they did. He was a guy who dealt in truth and fact. And the facts here were either not the truth or not the facts. Or neither, but that was impossible for Lou Mathews to consider. As far as his world view was concerned, there had to be an explanation he could fathom, and whatever the facts of this strange case might turn out to be, the lack of a reasonable explanation only exacerbated his concern for Carla.

Sliding the papers back in their oversized envelope, he grabbed his coat and headed for the door. He didn't want to leave these papers sitting around where someone might get snoopy and take a look. He hadn't even told his partner about this. Anyway, his partner had been out sick with the flu for over a week and might have to be hospitalized, last Lou heard. Seemed pneumonia was the latest worry. Poor guy was in terrible shape, smoked, drank, and never walked if he could ride. One of these days, Lou worried, they'd be in a situation when his health issues might put them both at risk.

Ah, well, he thought as he walked out into the cold, clean air, it wasn't like he was working vice anymore. Not too many shootouts in the kinds of cases he worked these days. This was more like a nest of hornets to smoke out, and if he was going to find a reasonable explanation, he figured it had to happen at Carla's restaurant. He turned in that direction as a noisy snow plow chugged by pushing mounds of snow out of its way, some of which added to the already steep pile on Lou's car.

Chapter Forty-Two

Eight o'clock seemed like it would never arrive, leaving Carla on edge all day. She was even short tempered with Raoul.

"What is wrong with you, girl?" he asked when she snapped at him about a pot of stew he'd left boiling on one of the stove burners. "Don't I know when my stew is done? You haven't got to tell me after all these years."

He looked at her with raised eyebrows, thinking she would take the cue and tell him what was going on, but she turned away as if she hadn't said a thing, wandered to the back and sat down at a table that hadn't been bussed yet. Raoul shook his head, mystified further by this completely out of character behavior. He motioned to one of the waitresses to clear the table and retreated to the kitchen.

At seven-thirty, Carla took her coat from the rack, picked up her purse, and opened the door. Whatever snow had melted was now crusty in the night air. Most of the sidewalks had been shoveled. Carla walked along with a steady, determined gait, her feet warm in winter boots, a scarf around her neck and gloves on her hands. As she breathed, clouds of vapor formed and then disappeared. The moon rose above the buildings, and the city was unusually quiet, normal sounds muffled by piles of snow with few cars or people about, so she had the streets almost to herself.

She wondered about Alanna and Joe. Would they be outside the house waiting for her? Were they real, or was it just some dream she had created because she needed a sign after all these years that the past was not going to haunt her forever? But they had led her to Moses, so it couldn't have been a dream. It's possible, she thought, that I'll never see them again, that they were just a momentary thing to bring me to my son and then— poof—they're gone. That was it, then. She was on her own, the way she'd been for most of her life.

She squared her shoulders and took a deep breath as the house came into view, its porch light on, steps clear of toys, looking almost inviting, and yet Carla had a feeling of despair, for if her son refused to acknowledge her, life as she'd always known it would cease. For a moment she thought of turning and running back to her own house, back to her life, to the certainty of the everyday routine she knew so well. But then there was no turning back in life. You had to move forward. There was no other way. That's what Lou Mathews had meant the other night. They had time. But only to go on, not to go back.

She rang the bell. Alanna and Joe were nowhere around. Or so she thought. Sometime earlier that afternoon, Morgan had appeared as they walked along a snowy street heading toward Doyle's, where Joe was convinced he would find the answer to what happened to his partner, Russ.

"I'm just saying it's futile for you to be so wrapped up in this," Alanna had said as they set out for the bar. "We're supposed to be granting wishes so we can figure out our own lives. What happened to your partner is immaterial to that."

"No, it isn't," he took her by the arm to emphasize his point. "The way I see it is everything's wrapped up together. Your fiancé, my partner, how we died . . ." He was about to say "or almost died" but stopped, because just down the block there was Morgan, looking like himself for once, leaning against a parking meter, as nonchalant as if he were just another city dweller waiting for a bus.

"Uh-oh," Alanna said. "What did we do?"

"Or what do we have to do? Boy, I could really use a not-drink right now."

"How about we use The Manifest and skip out on him." Alanna never thought she'd want to ditch Morgan, but now that Carla's wish was about to come true, she really wanted some time off. Some time to get things straight with Joe. They were always being wrenched apart by this situation, by the needs of others, by Morgan, and she was feeling edgy all the time lately. Time. That was their problem. They just needed some time by themselves.

"Great idea," Joe whispered in her ear. "I'd like nothing better than to dematerialize with you to a desert island for about two weeks and have no cares in the world—or out of the world. But he's spotted us."

"Well, you two. You're looking more like an old married couple every time I see you." Morgan spoke in that deep gravelly voice they knew so well by now.

"Morgan," Alanna spoke for both of them, "what are you doing out here? We've set everything up for Carla. Her wish is about to come true. We're almost done here."

"In a bit of a hurry, aren't you?" Morgan smiled and stepped away from his post by the parking meter. "Let's all go to Doyle's together. I think you'll find it's particularly hospitable this afternoon. And it's almost happy hour, so why not?"

"You're coming with us?" Joe asked. In fact, he was astonished. Morgan as a drinking buddy. It was an intriguing thought. Did Morgan know some great drinking games? Maybe the floating paper clip?

The bar was almost empty. It seemed snow kept customers home, and anyway, it was the middle of the week. Michael Doyle was stationed at a booth in the back playing solitaire, but as always, watching the scene. He glanced at the three of them when they walked in but saw nothing of note and went back to his cards.

Alanna had the feeling they were getting away with something. If only people knew. Sometimes she wanted to tell a stranger. Just pull someone off the street and say, "Hey. I'm not really here. But I am sort of here. And if you have a wish you want granted, I'm your girl."

A fantasy, for sure, but lately she'd been wondering what she would say when the time came to make her choice. Stay or go back. It was a choice that hadn't confused her in the beginning, but the more time she spent with Joe, the more confused she got.

Chapter Forty-Three

Moses opened the door, and for the first time in her life, ever since the day he was taken from her, before she even saw him as a newborn baby, Carla looked at the face of her child, now a grown man. He was taller than she thought he would be. And his skin was lighter, although she thought—it was only the most fleeting of thoughts, yet she was aware of it, and it stirred some deep wound in her— he would not be as dark as she was. What she felt was neither shame nor anger, but a kind of sadness that this had not been her choice of a father for her only son.

He had broad shoulders and stood with dignity and self-assurance. She could see no trace of arrogance in his demeanor, and for that she was grateful, for this had been her greatest fear, that he would have inherited from whichever of those boys had fathered him some of the bully, the sense of entitlement, the notion that taking was his right. But she saw none of it. She saw only a man who had responsibilities waiting to hear what she had to say. He had, she realized, the look of someone who could handle himself in any situation. This gave her a sense of relief as well, for Carla had troubled over what this news would do to him for so long that, in her mind, she had created someone who might feel threatened by her news.

He invited her in. They exchanged the usual pleasantries. She asked after his son, who had fallen on the porch. She heard giggling from the dining room and Cecilia telling the children to go upstairs and make sure they were well prepared for school tomorrow. Carla heard them tromping up the wooden steps, teasing each other. She heard dishes being stacked and the sound of running water coming from the kitchen.

"My wife said you had something to talk to me about," Moses began as he ushered Carla into the living room and motioned for her to sit on the couch while he took a large wing chair to her side.

It was the same spot where Carla had sat earlier in the day. She felt a wave of heat spread up from her chest to her neck and through her face. She shrugged out of her coat and held her handbag on her lap for something to steady herself.

"Yes," Carla said, "I do have something to tell you, and I'm afraid it might be causing you some shock after all these years."

She watched his face, but he was either unaware of the reason for her visit or he was the kind of person who didn't react right away. In any case, Carla felt she must push ahead, so she said, "It's about . . . well, it's about when you . . . when you were born." After she got it out, she sat back against the couch and took a breath. Her grip on her purse loosened.

"Have you come to tell me who my parents were?" Moses asked and then said, "because if you have, my parents were Vaneeta and Joseph Freeman."

"I know that," Carla said. "And I know that they were good parents and loved you."

"Yes, they were. And yes they did. And I loved them. And now they're gone, I'm not going to do anything to disturb their memory," he said.

"Then perhaps I should go," Carla said, hoping he would stop her, hoping he would relent.

But he did not. He was polite, even cordial. He showed her to the door and thanked her for coming. As she stepped beyond the door jamb onto the porch, she turned to him and said, "It's always better to know the truth. The truth can't hurt you but hiding can eat away at your soul. I know. I know firsthand."

She walked out, her purse over her arm, tears stinging her cheeks, and slowly, carefully descended the steps to the path and onto the sidewalk that was glistening a little under the light of a street lamp. It was what she had always feared. He would turn away. But, she told herself, that is his choice, and there's nothing I can do about it now. Wishing was fine in its way, but everyone had to face their own reality sometime, and Carla was no different. It didn't matter how many good works you did or how well and honestly you had lived your life. Everyone had a past, and everyone had to move forward in the shadow of that past.

*

Later that night, at the home of Moses and Cecilia Freeman, an argument began to rumble. It began when Moses asked Cecilia if she knew what that woman had wanted to see him about and why she hadn't told him straight up. Cecilia told Moses she didn't tell him because she didn't want to make up his mind for him, that it was his decision to make about what he wanted to know and when. She told him she had never been able to make sense of his feelings about his past and that she had always thought she would want to know who her mother was and why she gave up her baby. But she told him she respected his wishes because it was a very personal decision. It stopped there, but the next morning it started again.

This time he was somewhat belligerent, challenging Cecilia to tell him why he should want to know. Asking what gave her the right to judge him. Saying he had gone through all this years ago when he was a teenager, and it was behind him. Cecilia answered as calmly as she could that if it was really behind him, he wouldn't be so worked up about it. That there must be some anxiety for him, some quest he had denied, some need he had that was still unfulfilled. She said he couldn't hide from it forever and that this was the perfect opportunity to face it.

At the station, he reprimanded a rookie for not hanging up his gear properly. Then he yelled at one of the firemen on his team for having a sloppy locker. He tossed the man's personal things onto the floor and told him to clean up his mess. There was a sense at the fire station that something was bugging the captain, but no one said anything, instead cut a wide berth around him.

At home he was curt and short tempered, and finally Cecilia confronted him, saying he needed to put his house in order.

He threw a glass of apple juice against a kitchen wall, and for the first time in their married life he stormed out the door, coming back after midnight and crawling into bed. But Cecilia was awake, and when she heard him sigh deeply, thinking she was asleep, she turned to him and said she always thought she married a hero, a brave man who could face anything.

"What do you know about bravery?" he asked. "You sit in a schoolroom every day and talk about writers who've been dead for hundreds of years. I face death every time that bell rings. Your bells just mean it's lunch time or another group of kids is coming into your room. I know what courage is. And this ain't about courage, Cissy. You don't understand."

"Then explain it to me, Moses," Cecilia whispered in the dark. "Explain to me how you can have the kind of courage it takes to face those flames, and you can't talk to one old black lady and hear her side of the story. You explain that to me now."

208

"It's different, that's all," Moses said.

It took an hour of this back and forth, and finally Cecilia said the one thing he couldn't ignore.

"It's fine for you to make this decision for your life," she said. "But what about those two children of yours? Do you want them to feel the way you feel? And what happens if one day they find out they've got a grandmother living in the same city and their daddy didn't want to acknowledge her? Do you think they're going to be happy about that? Do you think that's going to be good for them?"

Chapter Forty-Four

"So, Joe what'll you have?" Morgan crooked his finger toward the bartender, who, without waiting for the order, brought two tall, dark-green glasses and set them down, one in front of Alanna and the other in front of Joe. Small curls of vapor rose from the glasses, while from out of nowhere a most pleasant scent filled the air.

"Ooh, what are these?" Alanna picked up her glass gingerly and sniffed the vapor. She smiled immediately and took a sip.

"You two have worked hard, and the Committee thinks you need a little R and R. This is just a start. Drink up. I'm sure you'll be pleasantly surprised." Morgan grinned at them.

"But what about Carla? We only brought her to the house. We don't know what happened once she went inside," Alanna said.

"Listen, if the Committee wants to give us a break, I say we take it and no questions asked." Joe picked up his glass and drank a good bit of it down in one long gulp.

"That's the ticket, Joe," said Morgan. "You know how to make the best of a situation."

Joe nodded and drank the rest from the dark-green glass. "Hey, this is good. Almost like a not-drink, but not a not-drink. I mean, I don't remember it being so spicy. And . . ."

"And what, Joe?"

"I know what you mean," chimed in Alanna. "This has a peculiar aftertaste. Like candy almost. But with a slight tang. Or perfume. I don't know what to make of it."

"What do you want to make of it?" asked Morgan. But he knew they were not listening to him anymore.

They were traveling now. Whirling in space like feathers cast about on the wind. Joe took Alanna's hand as they floated and twirled like cosmic dancers until they slowly descended to a meadow by a lake. Huge trees surrounded them, and the lake was a dark blue with a silvery mirror sheen.

"What is this place?" Alanna asked. "What was in that drink?"

"I don't know, but I think the drink was some sort of transporter."

Before Alanna could say anything else, Joe took her other hand and pulled her to him. They were alone now, and it seemed to him he'd been waiting forever to take her in his arms. When they kissed, she did not resist, did not even think about what could happen or about their mission or anything else but being here with Joe, in this moment, together.

It seemed like forever before they released from their embrace, and when they did, Joe stroked her hair and said, "If only we could stay here forever. Would you like that?"

"Yes," Alanna whispered and tilted her chin up for another kiss.

At that moment there was a rumbling, like thunder, way off in the distance, and the ground under their feet shook.

"What's that?" Joe peered across the lake to where the water had begun to move toward them in a wave from the far shore. Where they stood at the edge of the lake began to crumble, and they jumped back as the earth fell away into the water.

"Joe, look," Alanna pointed to the treetops.

Above them a dark cloud had formed, and the treetops swayed.

"We've got to get out of here," Joe said as the wind picked up and the wave approached from the opposite shore, faster now.

Holding her hand, he took off toward a steep hill behind them, running as fast as he could without losing Alanna.

"Where are you going?" she yelled, for now the wind howled and she could feel a mist against her skin as the water roiled behind them.

"I think there's a cave up there. If we can get to it, we can ride out the storm."

They scrambled and stumbled uphill, branches and brambles scratching against Alanna's bare legs, for she was wearing only a dress and boots. Pebbles fell off behind them, cascading down and down. Making pinging noises as they hit larger rocks and ledges. Joe held tight to Alanna's hand for fear she might slide back. When she did, he stopped and pulled her up beside him, and they plodded up and up until they reached the cave.

"How did you see this way up here?" Alanna asked as they squeezed through the narrow opening.

"I don't know. Somehow I just knew it was here."

They stopped just inside the opening. Near the entrance the light was dim, but farther back they could see a shaft of light from an opening in the top of the cave. Above the opening was a thick rock ledge protecting the inside from the rain but allowing light to enter. Outside thunder boomed in great clapping cracks, and now lightning flashed ominously, but with each flash they could see that the cave was large, and behind them was a thick green carpet of fresh moss, fed by a trickling of water from somewhere beyond and above the cave. Inside the air was heavy and fresh like a forest after a spring rain.

"Come, let's wait it out on that moss." Joe suggested. And then, as he looked at Alanna, he saw her legs were scratched badly from the climb.

212

He led her to the moss and made her lie down. Her body sank into it, and she was surprised at how thick and luxurious it was, amazed that simple moss could be such a wonderful bed.

He took out his handkerchief and held it under the trickle of water until it was dripping. He applied it to her scratches, wiping them clean of debris and blood. He did this over and over until the cuts were clean.

"You're very sweet, Joe," she whispered in a voice full of emotion. He turned to her and leaned down.

"So are you," he said as he kissed her lips and ran his hand down her arm. "The sweetest thing I've ever seen. I want you more than I've ever wanted anything or anyone. I wish we could stay here forever. I wish this storm would never end and the drink would never wear off."

He unbuttoned her blouse and touched her breast and after that, the storm raged around them but they couldn't have said how long it lasted or how it ended, only that this cave, this moss, this moment was delicious in every excruciating detail.

Chapter Forty-Five

It was barely eight o'clock. Michael Doyle sent Tempest home early because of the snow. He said there wasn't enough business beyond the bar to keep her serving tables, so she trudged off, shivering because her coat was too thin for this kind of cold and she'd forgotten her gloves and scarf. Carla had said something about taking her to the mission to search for a warmer coat but had been too distracted lately to follow up on that plan.

She muttered as she walked briskly to Carla's house, imagining the warm kitchen and her bedroom. She liked heat. In fact, needed heat. It was a damn shame she'd spent so much time in cold climates lately, and she couldn't wait to get done here and move on.

Maybe tonight she would get into that locked room. She felt in her coat pocket for the large paper clip she'd swiped from Michael Doyle's desk. It was impossible to sneak into the cash drawer tonight with the place so empty. She was thinking about how little money she had left and what she would need to pay off Benny Fingers and have some left over to get out of town. She'd like to go in style. She'd arrived on a bus. Not her choice. She'd been strapped for cash even then. It wasn't fair. She'd done everything that had been asked of her. The rewards were supposed to be there, waiting. Soon, she figured, she'd be on easy street, or at least fancy street. She'd had it good in London. It seemed like a long time ago, and she resented that she had to stoop to stealing to get money.

She had worked herself up into quite a little snit by the time she reached Carla's house and let herself in through the side kitchen door. Snow still covered the backyard, and Marv had shoveled only a narrow path from the street to the door. Tempest looked up for a second before turning the key. On a bright, clear night like this almost anything could happen.

She passed the hooks where everyone in the house always hung their coats and noted that Marv's and Carla's were both missing. That meant Bugs was probably out with Marv, as well, but there was no telling how long before they would be back. She decided now was the time anyway and headed straight for that locked door.

If Carla had hoped to make this a room safe from prying eyes or possible thievery, she would have been sorely disappointed. It took Tempest only a few moments of fiddling with the straightened paper clip, her ear close to the lock so she could hear the click of the tumblers, to snap it open and bingo! She was turning the knob and entering the forbidden room. What she found there was ordinary in every way—at least what she could see at first glance.

She switched on the light after closing the door behind her. Furnished simply, with an old wooden desk and chair opposite the door, a faded upholstered wingback chair in the far corner and, covering almost every spare inch of wall space, bookshelves from floor to ceiling literally stuffed, crammed, overflowing with volumes of every height, width, color, binding, age, and texture. They were packed so tightly into the shelves that some books protruded far out, making the walls look like a bricklaying job gone haywire.

Tempest didn't know what to make of it or where to begin. A needle in a haystack would be easy compared to this, she thought. At least she would know she was looking for a needle. She began at one wall at the bottom near the floor, searching each book for a title. Some were so old and worn the covers were frayed and impossible to read on the spine. Others were stuck in the shelves backwards so she couldn't see their spines at all. If she could stay in this room openly for a few days, she thought, maybe she could find the right book. The whale of a book. What could that mean, she wondered again as she scanned the shelves.

And then an idea struck her. She would go to Carla and offer to clean the whole house top to bottom. As a way to repay Carla's kindness. Carla couldn't refuse. She would consider it an insult to refuse someone wanting to do something in return for a kindness. And Tempest could ask about this room. She could talk Carla into letting her clean it, too. And when she saw it for the first time—Carla wouldn't know she'd already seen it— she could offer to arrange the books in some order, perhaps by size or alphabetically. Yes, that was the perfect plan to allow her unlimited access. She shut the door, pushing the lock in to be sure she left it the way she'd found it.

*

Detective Lou Mathews sat opposite Benny Fingers in the dim light of an interrogation room, as confident as a man who's just drawn to an inside straight. He smiled as he leaned forward and pressed the little button on the mini digital recorder. Out came Benny's voice, and then Elaine's. Benny's head drooped a little, swagger replaced by capitulation. Benny was a man who knew how to figure odds. And the odds were dead set against him.

"So," he asked, raising his head. "What are you after?"

"Well," Lou Mathews smiled, "I've already got you on conspiracy. And your co-conspirator implicates you as the

216

trigger puller. You killed an officer of the court, you know. Judges and juries don't much like to hear about a lawyer gunned down in front of his own office. Makes them feel unsafe, as if the world has gone sort of off kilter. And you don't cut a very sympathetic figure."

"Uh huh," Benny Fingers grunted, thinking, this cop wants something or he'd have thrown me into a cell already.

"You're right, Benny," Detective Mathews mumbled. "Tell me it wasn't you who pulled that trigger, and we'll take your girlfriend down and give you some . . ." he thought for a minute and then said, "consideration."

"What kind of consideration?"

"Well, I think the district attorney might see clear to a fifteen-year stretch on the conspiracy with a parole recommendation. Of course, you'd have to convince us that she was the shooter."

"How can I convince you of that?"

"Maybe you kept the gun with her fingerprints on it?"

Benny chuckled. "You must think we're both stupid. That gun is gone forever. I only told her I still had it to get what I wanted out of her. You get my drift?"

Benny leaned back, a smirk on his face. "But I might have something else for you. That is, if you were to knock that fifteen to eight, parole in five. For a deal like that, I think I could scratch up something you'd find interesting."

"And what would that be?"

"See, it's this way, detective. I got this hobby. I just love to make videos with a hidden camera. I'm kinda like what you might call a candid-camera producer. Like on TV, you know?"

Detective Mathews nodded. "And what about the partner?"

"Partner? What're you talking about? It was just me and her. All the way. See, I got this thing for blondes and when she came to me with the deal, I couldn't say no. I was retired at that point and only got back in the game because of her."

He shrugged like a man in thrall to an irresistible urge in the form of blonde, buxom, Elaine, the chorus girl from Vegas, and all of a sudden, he looked to Lou Mathews like just another poor sap who'd gotten himself snookered by a woman. Then Lou thought about Carla. Not all women were like that, he was thinking when Benny brought him back to the here and now.

"Are you telling me she had a partner?" Benny asked, his voice rising with anger.

"No, nothing like that. I'm talking about the lawyer's partner. Who put the hit on him. And why? I mean, she was in it for the insurance money. But what was the percentage on the partner?"

"Listen, detective, if there was anything else, why would I hold it back now? I got nothing about a partner. All I heard about him was a truck collided with his car and he got his in the accident. But that's all it was. An accident. You can't pin that on me or her. It was just coincidence. Fate. You know? Just his destiny, I guess."

So, Lou Mathews thought, the guy who looks like the partner must just be some damn look alike and nothing more. Hard to accept, but there it was. He was dead and gone. And this guy hanging around Doyle's was nothing more than a guy. Still, it was puzzling, but he had long ago accepted that not all puzzles can be solved, and maybe this was just going to be one of them. And now that he had this case as neatly packaged as a Valentine's box of chocolate, there was just one other thing.

"What about the girl?" he asked. "Where does she fit in?"

Chapter Forty-Six

Carla walked home in the dark along shoveled, salted sidewalks, a lonely figure against traffic signals that cast eerie alternately red, yellow, or green reflections on the empty streets. It was easy, she thought, to feel alone in a crowd, but it was even lonelier on a night like this when everyone was safely tucked away inside their warm homes. He didn't want to know her. That's all she could think about, all she could see, all she could conjure. He was satisfied with what he knew, and he didn't need anything more.

Carla didn't weep. She didn't fume and fuss. She didn't feel cheated. A kind of numbness entered her heart, and what had happened all those decades ago became like a cement block, immovable, solid, forever fixed.

Alanna and Joe were nowhere to be seen, and she didn't even think their absence was worthy of anger or regret. They had come to grant her wish. They had done their work and now they were gone. Or had she dreamt it all? It all seemed unreal now, even more than it had before. And even though she knew she hadn't dreamed it, now that the hope and expectation they had filled her with was gone, it did seem like a dream now. A dream she could not put out of her mind.

She walked the last steps to her house and opened the front door just in time to see Tempest disappearing up the stairs. So, she thought, the girl is not at work tonight. Maybe I dreamt her, too, Carla thought wryly. Maybe everything in life is a dream, like Shakespeare wrote. A dream from which you wake for a few moments before going back to your dream state, where you can live and work and move about without the pain that comes from losing something you never really had.

Carla stood there, just inside the door, for she could not impel herself up the stairs, nor remove herself from the spot by the door, as if half expecting a call that would beckon her back to the house she had recently left, back to the son she had recently found, back to a future she had hoped for but that would now be bleaker for its emptiness. And then, behind her, another key jiggled in the lock, and there were Marv and Bugs, coming in from their nighttime walk.

Bugs hustled up to her, his tail wagging happily, thumping against her legs. He sniffed at her hand and stuck his cold nose into her fingertips and then . . . then, when she needed someone to love and care for her, when she needed affirmation more than she had ever needed it, he licked her hand and whined softly in a way that melted her heart. She leaned down and cradled his head in her hands.

"Bugs, you old boy, you know when a body's in need of caring, don't you?"

Bugs slumped against her heavily and would not budge from the spot.

"Bugsy," Marv called and patted his leg to bring the dog away from Carla. But Bugs did not move, and Marv knew something was up.

He stood there waiting for Carla to say something, but she just hugged Bugs to her and Bugs did not move.

"Carla," Marv said after a few moments. "I have something to say to you. I should have said it before but I haven't seen you at all. And now, well, now seems like not a good time. Is something wrong? Something I can help you with?"

"I don't expect there's much to do," Carla answered softly. "I expect I'm just getting older. A lot of things in life you simply got to accept. Ain't that so, Bugs?" She rubbed the dog's head, and his tail thumped again.

"You're right about that," Marv agreed. "and I've been thinking, you know, as much as you've done for me, for all these years, I want to thank you. And for what happened here, with the girl, I want to say I'm sorry. I don't know what else to say. I've gone back to AA, and that's the best I can do. Except to tell you it's time I was moving out on my own. I've been staying here because I was afraid of what I might do if I got sidetracked. But now I see I could get sidetracked anywhere by anyone, and it's up to me to make sure that doesn't happen. I have to . . . you know . . . be independent finally. I hope you understand. And I hope you know you can always call on me for anything you need. Anytime."

Carla didn't say anything for a few moments, and Marv waited. Finally she cupped Bugs by his chin and said to the dog, "You go on to Marv now, boy. You take good care of him. Because you and he are my favorite folks in this world." She pushed the dog gently toward Marv, and they both climbed the stairs slowly, without looking back.

*

"We should have walked with her," Alanna told Joe. "She looked so sad. How could Morgan let this happen?"

"More to the point, what are we supposed to do now? This is hardly what I would call a granted wish. If it's what I had wished for, it sure isn't what I would have wanted to happen."

They followed along as far as Carla's house and then stopped. Joe reached out and placed his hand around the back of Alana's neck and leaned down to kiss her, but she pulled back.

221

"What?" he said, teasing and tried again.

"Hey, wait a sec," she shook her head. "We've got to concentrate."

"I am concentrating."

Alanna sighed and took Joe's hand. "Look, just because . . . well, you know what . . . we can't forget what we're here to do. I just feel this mission is not over yet. And while we're still not done, I think we've got to stick to the job and not get sidetracked."

"We already did get sidetracked. And if I'm not mistaken, you were not exactly an unwilling participant. I don't see any harm in us continuing with some R and R, as Morgan so aptly put it, even while we're on the job, as you so aptly put it."

He leaned down before she could object and kissed her. When he pulled away, satisfied that she wanted the same thing he did, he smiled at her and put his arm around her shoulders.

"That's better, isn't it? I mean, we're really getting somewhere now."

Alanna shrugged and leaned her body against him in a way she hadn't before. "I can't fight you anymore. You're right. This is different."

"So maybe you'll forget about that stuffed shirt of a fiancé and agree to come back with me when we're all done with this wish-granting business."

"I don't know, Joe. I just don't think it's that simple."

"Let's go have another whatever-they-were-drinks, and maybe we'll catch up with Morgan again so we can ask him what's next."

They passed Carla's house, not realizing what was going on inside, not knowing that Tempest had already gone to Carla's room, proposed her plan to Carla, who, in her emotionally weakened state and trusting as her nature was, said she had been

222

meaning to straighten out the house and especially that room herself for years, and it would be so kind of Tempest to do it for her and what a sweet child she was after all.

Chapter Forty-Seven

Now that Tempest had free access to the room where she was sure she'd find that hidden treasure, she got some other good news. Benny Fingers had been arrested. She heard it at work. Also, he was singing his lungs out, according to Michael Doyle, who was unusually chatty about the whole thing. Tempest didn't have a clue why and didn't care. That eliminated both Benny and the blonde woman, who Tempest had suspected was going to be a problem, more for Benny than for anyone else.

If he wanted to retire, fine, but teaching someone else the tricks of the trade meant putting himself at her mercy. It was just not good to get emotionally involved with clients. But then Tempest had only one client. When you worked for the Devil, you were answering only to him, and emotional involvement was not an issue. Now, whatever money or anything else she discovered in that room was hers alone.

To make it look good, she did start cleaning the house—albeit lackadaisically—from the top. There was another bedroom and bath on her floor, and that was as good a place to start as any. On the floor below, she came to Marv's rooms. Since he'd been there so long, Marv had a bedroom, bathroom, and study, where he had a drafting table and computer. There was a dog bed on the floor where Bugs slept and plants on a stand in front of the window. Poor Marv, Tempest thought, although there was no empathy in her mind for the man, you just want to be a homebody, don't you?

She smiled at the thought of his hands on her thigh and at how easy it was to get him drinking. If she had more time, she thought, she'd like to really pull him down. She shrugged it off.

Her objective was clear, and getting Marv back on the sauce was too easy and would yield her few points.

Marv still liked to draw his plans by hand with a drafting pencil on paper and then transfer the finished work to a CAD file. It was more tedious, but he was in no hurry and only wanted to do the best work possible for his customers. He'd lost so many years that now he aimed to make every bit of work count. Stacks of papers littered the desk, all neatly piled and labeled. With a duster in her hand, Tempest glanced at the scribbles that looked to her like a lot of nothing. She dusted the desk and moved to the drafting table, where she looked down at a plan labeled "Connor Addition & Restoration." Below that was an address, not three blocks away. So that's where Marv spent his time when he wasn't in the house or walking that mangy Bugs.

She dusted around the edges of the desk and was about to move on to the floor lamp when her gaze rested on a note in the top right corner of the sheet. The note, written in neat lowercase above what looked like an enlargement of a smaller area along one line of the drawing, read "clandestine wall safe." Next to that was a smaller note that said "A Tale of Two Cities." Tempest leaned over the drawing to study it more closely.

As she followed the lines of the drawing, she realized this was a floor plan for a room in a house. And where the note met the line must have been a wall, and just like that, it clicked. Marv, that jokester of an old drunk, was designing wall safes in houses behind what looked on the outside like some classic old book. "Whale of a book" he had mumbled. A whale.

Tempest suddenly looked up at the ceiling, and her lips curled in a grin of triumph. It was a book that had something to do with whales. No wait. It was a big book about whales. Or a big book about a big whale. It must be, she thought. She dropped the duster and ran down the steps to the room crammed with books.

Now she could come and go freely. Carla had even unlocked the door. She rushed in and switched on the light. Once again, surrounded by hundreds of books crammed into every space, she began at one end of the room, searching, searching, reading titles, touching book covers, pulling books out as others tumbled down. This was maddening. It could be anywhere, any book, any shape, any size. Or maybe it was a book with its guts cut out and money stuffed inside in place of the pages. She spun around and around, growing ever more confused by all the books, and then it occurred to her that the perfect place to hide something was in plain sight surrounded by hundreds of the very same thing.

Again she smiled, but this was an evil little smile. She would figure this out. She always won in the end.

*

Benny Fingers not only ratted out Elaine in order to save his own skin, he gave Detective Mathews an in-depth look at the business side of getting rid of a problem. Only thing he couldn't figure out was how that cop got him on tape. And then he figured out that Michael Doyle must be playing both sides of the street. Gambling in the back room that the cops ignored for some consideration at the tables out front, consideration in the form of strategically placed listening bugs.

Oh, well, Benny thought, I got some cash put away for a rainy winter, and when I get out, I'll still be young enough to enjoy my retirement in sunny Miami. In this business, you had

226

to accept a certain risk-reward percentage. But broads, he told himself, they'll get you in trouble a hundred percent of the time.

Benny Fingers wasn't the only one trying to figure out the loose ends of this deal. For Lou Mathews, there was still a nagging question about that lawyer. It kept him awake at night staring into the darkness. When he was a kid, he'd heard that everyone has a double somewhere, and he wondered then if it could be true. But that was just kid stuff, and you'd never have convinced him of it now.

Still . . . it nagged at him like a cold sore. And then Carla's face and her sweet, throaty voice would come to him in his half-sleep state, and he would smile and drift off. That was how it should be with a woman. Just the thought of her should calm a man down and make him feel like he was right with the world.

In the morning, he was at the restaurant early for his fresh hot coffee and muffin warm from the oven. Raoul waved from behind the kitchen door before he disappeared to the back to check on the day's fresh deliveries. By now, Raoul had accepted Detective Mathews, even come to trust him. And then again, he watched Carla going through whatever was disturbing her soul, and he thought, she needs a good man. Needs someone, after all these years. So he let go the reins and left nature alone to take its course.

When Carla didn't come over to sit with him, Lou Mathews picked up his plate and mug and moved to the back, to the side booth where she sat alone, staring out the window past the orchids in bloom, to the street where a warming spell had melted the snow and cars and buses now moved freely.

"Like some company this morning?" he asked as he slid into the booth across from her.

"Oh," she jumped, jolted out of her reverie.

"Where were you?"

"When?"

"Just then. Staring out the window. Where'd you go to?"

Carla shrugged. How could she tell him?

"Something happen?"

She shrugged again and shook her head as if to say she wouldn't—or couldn't—tell him.

"That bad, huh?"

"Look, Lou," Carla began, but before she could say anything else, he reached over and took her hand in his.

"I know something is troubling you, and it's a heavy burden. Raoul knows it, too. We both love you. And accept you. And want you to be happy. But more than that, I want you to know that there is nothing, absolutely nothing on this Earth that could, or ever would, change my feelings for you. You can tell me or not. You can hide it for the rest of your life. But I'll be here. No matter what. Always." He squeezed her hand and she twined her fingers in his.

"Thank you, Lou. One day. When I feel stronger. One day I will tell you everything. But I can't right now. I just can't. Only be patient with me is all I need right now."

Chapter Forty-Eight

"See, everything's going to be all right. And we didn't even need Morgan." Alanna pointed at the restaurant window.

"Yeah, so let's go back to Doyle's and see if we can get another one of those whatever-drinks that Morgan hooked us up with before."

"Joe, it's eight in the morning. That bar won't be open now. And anyway—"

"Anyway then, let's go back to the B & B and get us some rest. I feel like I've been going for months."

"I know what you're thinking, Joe, and it's not about rest."

"So," he shrugged. "Blame a guy for trying. Anyway, Carla doesn't need us anymore."

As he spoke, a bus stopped at the curb right where they stood, and out stepped a dapper-looking man. Even though the weather had warmed, he wore a camel-hair overcoat and an old-fashioned fedora on his head, and he held a silver-handled walking stick, which he twirled slightly before he stepped off the bus. Using the cane almost as a dance prop, he walked over to the bookstore next to Carla's Home Cooking and gazed intently at the window display, which was an impressive array of books in all shapes and sizes covering just about anything of interest to anyone. After more than a few seconds, he turned his head toward Alanna and Joe in such a way that they felt compelled to stare back at him, and when they did, they realized who it was. With his cane held in one hand, he beckoned to them to come over.

"You show up at the oddest times," Joe began, but Morgan put a finger to his lips and pointed at the window.

"Ever wonder what really happens in a fairy tale?" he asked.

"Personally, I never went in for them myself," Joe mumbled, but Morgan was looking at Alanna.

She chuckled. "What are you referring to?"

"Take a look," he raised his cane, and with a wave of it across the wide window pane, one of the books opened in front of them, and as its pages ruffled, the book grew larger until it filled the entire window display. Inside there was a beautiful lawn and a gathering of many people, seated in rows, all dressed in spring clothes, the ladies wearing hats, the men jackets and ties. There was an aisle between the chairs, and down the aisle a bride walked holding the arm of an older man.

"It's a wedding. What's fairy tale about that?" Alanna asked.

"Let's turn the page and find out," Morgan said. With a wave of his cane the page turned.

"Oh, no," Alanna cried out. She looked around to see if anyone had heard her, but the people walking by were oblivious to them, as if they couldn't be seen.

"What?" Joe asked.

"It's him."

"Him who?" Joe started to say more but suddenly realized that the groom in this fairy tale must be Alanna's fiancé from—well, he couldn't really define how long it had been, for time had no meaning anymore now that they were living in Transition.

"Bradley Covington." Morgan said it in a whisper, as if he wanted only Alanna to hear him. "We've been watching him."

"I'm sorry, Alanna." Joe turned to Morgan. "Why'd you have to show her that?"

"I thought she'd like to know." He looked at Alanna and smiled a little. "Was I wrong?"

230

"I'm in shock, that's all," she said. "I just never imagined him moving on to someone else so fast."

"Has it been fast?"

They both looked at Morgan, and Joe asked, "How long has it been?"

"Does it really matter? The point is, life moves on and so must you. Your work here is almost done. I would caution you to stay close to Carla tonight. There are forces aligned against her that must be thwarted. After that, after Carla's wish is fully granted, you two will have to make your own wish. I won't see you again, but know this: I will be there when you need me. And the Committee is awaiting your decision."

With that, he tapped his cane against the window, and the books came back into view and everything was as it had been, except that the bus was gone, Morgan was gone, and Alanna and Joe simply dematerialized.

*

Detective Mathews wanted to speak to the girl, Tempest, but she didn't show up for work that night and Michael Doyle said she'd asked for the night off. It being a Wednesday, he gave it to her gladly. The bar was nearly empty, although the backroom game was going strong, so he didn't worry about the take. He wouldn't miss that blonde bimbo or Benny Fingers, and really, that girl Tempest was too skinny to sell enough drinks to make it worth keeping her on much longer. Next time he'd have to hire one with more curves.

Lou Mathews thought about taking her down to the precinct to question her, but he had nothing on her really.

Benny had said she hired him to pretend to attack him. He could get her on filing a false police report, except that she didn't call the police, so technically she didn't file the report. And, if he did arrest her, that would come back to Carla, who did file the report. He didn't want that. So he was stymied. Yet he couldn't figure out what that girl was up to. None of it made sense. He could understand if she wanted to get a job with Carla so she could steal from the till. But that hadn't happened, and as far as he knew, she had wanted to work at Doyle's from the start. Except for the few times Tempest had lifted a ten or twenty from the cash drawer as a tip, no one stole from Michael Doyle. Not with his connections. So what was her game?

He had planned to walk Carla home from the restaurant, but it was still too early, so he headed over to the station to finish up some paperwork. He'd meet with her later. And maybe she would open up about what was bothering her. He thought about taking her over to his place. But maybe it was too soon for that. Nothing was clear to him tonight. At least it was warming up and the snow was gone. That was something anyway.

Chapter Forty-Nine

Flames licked the edge of the curtains, crawling up toward the window, at first slowly, smoldering, creating a smoky haze between wall and fabric. Tempest watched with glee, her lips curled in an ugly smile as she clutched the big book with the gold-lettered title on the spine. *Moby Dick*, it read, and she smiled at that, too, for she should have put it together right away. That Marv. Even drunk he made a kind of sense.

She'd figured it out pretty fast once it came to her what he must have meant. A book that wasn't a book. A whale of a book that was really about a whale. A big book—big enough to hold twenty thousand dollars. Marv knew it was there all along and he hadn't taken it. What a fool, she thought. What a stupid, silly, old fool. He'd made the book especially for this purpose. Made it out of a heavy, old-leather binding wrapped and glued around what was really a strong box. It fit neatly into a specially constructed wall crevice. Not even locked. That's how sure he'd been that no one would ever figure it out.

At one point in her search, Tempest thought maybe this room held other treasures. Maybe that's why Carla kept it locked. But she hadn't found anything, and she was in a hurry now to move on. She'd leave no trace behind and that was satisfying in itself. An old clock on the back wall read 10:30. Not too late, but late enough.

She wished Marv was upstairs, too, but he and Bugs had left today, his personal stuff crammed into a rented SUV, that dog slinking past her with one last suspicious growl. He planned to move the rest over the weekend, he'd said. Yes, she wished he was in the house, asleep upstairs like Carla was, about to meet his fate like Carla was.

What luck that Carla had come home so early, said she was dead tired and was going to sleep. She looked sad, Tempest thought, and vaguely wondered why. Not that she cared. She hoped Carla would take a sleeping pill. She'd never gone to bed this early before. Tempest hoped for that anyway, but really, it didn't matter.

Smoke will immobilize her before she can call for help, and this old house will go up fast, Tempest thought. Old wood and old framing make for good kindling. She laughed to herself and headed for the door, already dressed in her thin coat and boots. Everything else, all the clothes and personal things Carla had provided for her, all the things she'd bought with her meager paycheck, all left upstairs to burn. All she needed was this book with its hidden stash, plenty to keep her going for a long while.

The room was getting hot. The curtains were shredding to ash now, and flames licked at the window sill and floorboards. The rug crackled and suddenly burst into flame. It wouldn't be long now. Nothing could stop it. Tempest took one last look around, spotted the disposable lighter she'd used to ignite the turpentine-soaked rags that she'd tossed under the curtains, grabbed it, and stuffed it into her pocket before turning away from the heat and heading out the door. She left the room open to allow the flames to spread more easily up the stairs.

Out on the street, she didn't wait to see the house go up but walked quickly toward the subway. She'd disappear soon enough. Before she turned the corner, she did take one long last look back. She could see an orange glow through one of the downstairs windows. Her smile turned to an icy sneer. And within a few seconds, the soft pale skin of her face thickened as creases showed under the makeup, and her nails turned green

234

while her spine curved in a slight arc to one side. No longer was she Tempest, the pretty, slender, waif in need of protection.

*

Earlier that day, after Lou Mathews left the restaurant, Carla sat by the window, unaware of what was happening around her. It was so unlike her that Raoul came out from the kitchen and asked if she was sick.

"No," she answered. "Not so you could send me to a doctor, anyway."

"What happened yesterday? You been moping around about something, and now you come and set here and do nothing and say nothing. This ain't like you. I got to tell you, it ain't natural. Now, either you tell me what it is, or you go talk to someone about it. How about that nice detective you been seeing?"

"You know about that?" Carla perked up for a moment.

"Hah." Raoul laughed and sat down, wiping his hands on his apron. It was almost time to open for the supper crowd, but so far the restaurant was closed to customers.

"I been watching you two. He surely likes you. And you surely like him. Now, what you gonna do about it? You gonna let yourself get all bottled up so's you chase him off? You got a chance here, girl. Take it and run."

It was good advice and Carla appreciated it, but the tear in her soul had nothing to do with Lou Mathews and wasn't something he could fix.

She sighed and sat up straighter. "You're right, my good friend. You're always right. I just need a little time to get over a hurt I got put on me last night. I was hoping for something and it didn't work out, and so I just have to set it right in my mind. It's a lot to accept. And it makes me feel awfully blue. But I'll get back to normal. I promise you I will."

"Long as you do, that's okay by me. You take the time you need. Just remember, there's folks out here who care about you."

"I guess I have to accept that change doesn't always come the way you expect it to," Carla said. "But I appreciate my friends, and you know you're more than that to me. You're the brother I never had, the good soul who's always there, the rock I lean on when the wind blows hard across my face."

"You go on home now and take some time for yourself. You rest and stop all this thinking about what you can't change no way, and you'll feel like yourself in no time. Go on now." He stood up and reached out his hand to help her stand.

Carla looked up and smiled at him, realizing that she was lucky in so many ways that to let herself wallow in disappointment would do no one any good, least of all her. You never knew what tomorrow was going to bring. There was no reason to give up hope on her son. Maybe, just maybe, one day he would come around. She wouldn't live her life for that day, but she wouldn't rule it out either. At least she knew he was healthy and happy with a wonderful family and a solid life. She sure would love to spoil those two boys, though. Yes, she sure would. She felt tired all of a sudden, the way a person who's struggled with a dilemma feels worn out after finally coming to a conclusion, as if at the end of a long race.

Chapter Fifty

"She left hours ago, she was that wore out," Raoul told the detective. "You want some supper? I got some real nice chicken cacciatore back in the kitchen."

Lou Mathews shook his head. "Thanks anyway, Raoul. I grabbed a bite with a couple of the guys at the station while I was finishing up some paperwork. Why was she so worn out?"

"Won't say. Won't say nothing." He shook his head and shrugged. "Don't seem right, her being so closed. Not like her. Usually she's so . . . you know . . . friendly and open. No sir, not like her at all."

"Maybe I should give her a call."

"Said she was going to sleep for the rest of the night and long as it took for her to get to feeling like herself."

The detective in Lou Mathews couldn't let this alone. I can't go over there and pound on her door, he thought. But something is wrong, and if I don't do something, I'll just sit up all night worrying about her.

"So this is what love feels like," he actually muttered as he slipped his arms back into his coat.

"What's that?" Raoul asked. He'd heard something but just couldn't make out the words.

"Oh, nothing. I was just talking to myself."

"Better watch that, detective. When a man start to talk to himself, you know he got it bad. Real bad." Raoul laughed as he walked back to check that the ovens were all turned off and the kitchen was being cleaned up properly.

Right, Lou Mathews thought to himself. I do have it bad. He shook his head and opened the door. The cold had passed and the night had a hint of spring about it. Leaving his overcoat unbuttoned, he turned to walk toward Carla's house and bumped smack into Joe, who at that moment had turned away from the bookstore window, leaving Alanna staring inside at the book Morgan had opened for her earlier that day.

The bookstore was closed now. But she couldn't get that image out of her mind. Brawley marrying some other girl. Brawley moving on with his life. What had she expected? They must have assumed she was dead. That's what happens when a person disappears and no body is found. People just assume it's over and move on. People have to live. After all, life is meant for the living. Except for us, she was thinking at that moment. For us, life is . . . what?

She was about to turn to ask Joe what he thought it meant when, inside the window display, one of the books began to curl at the edges. She watched, fascinated, as the edges crinkled and turned black and tiny flames licked at the edges, and she thought . . . yes, she heard a scream, like the silent scream when you have a nightmare and you think you're screaming, but it's only in your mind, or in that part of your mind that's working overtime, separated from the part of your mind that's still sleeping, and you can't awaken to stop the scream until finally you are screaming out loud and waking in a sweat.

The book was burning gaily now, almost laughing at her as she stared into the window. The scream was softer, farther away, and as Alanna turned, she realized what it meant, and there was Joe, bumping into that detective and she felt rather than thought, in a way you feel something in your gut without needing a logical explanation, that something was wrong. Horribly wrong.

"Joe," she called out. Both men turned to her.

"You're getting to be a regular fixture around here, aren't you?" Detective Mathews said to Joe. He put a hand on Joe's shoulder, more to show a kind of camaraderie than intimidation.

"Won't be here too much longer," Joe answered rather enigmatically, and as Lou Mathews was about to ask what he meant, Alanna ran to them.

"We've got to go. Come on." She took Joe's hand and pulled him away.

"What's the rush?"

"Something's wrong with Carla."

"How do you know?"

"I saw something in the bookstore window. Something bad. Hurry," she dragged him along until he was running beside her, still clutching her hand.

Lou Mathews heard, and he followed as they ran down the street, hand in hand, like two children running from the scene of a mishap. When he caught up, he overtook them and stopped, effectively blocking their path.

"Wait a second." He held up his hands. "What's going on? What do you two know about Carla? And who are you anyway?" He glared at Joe, suspicious all over again.

"There's no time!" Alanna screamed at him. "Get out of the way!" She maneuvered past Lou Mathews, and they took off running again, this time as fast as they could go.

"Where are we running?" Joe asked, a bit out of breath now. He hadn't been to a gym since the car crash and had no idea how long it had been.

"Her house!" Alanna yelled to him.

"Why don't we just materialize there? That would be faster." He pulled her into a doorway and hugged her close so they would dematerialize together, and just as Detective

Mathews reached them, they faded away like a cold mist, and he was left staring in utter disbelief and asked once again, "Who was this guy?"

But there was no time now to mull it over. The worry over Carla intensified, and he ran down the street toward her house. Two blocks and he turned left, ran another two blocks and turned right, then ran the last block until he saw the church on the corner and swung around, feet pounding on the sidewalk, with no one else out this late, and there it was, the front stoop, and he could already smell the smoke hanging in the still air and his heart pounded harder, not just from the run, but with fear.

"Carla!" he yelled out as he pulled his phone from his pocket and hit the button that went directly to his precinct. The sergeant picked up and the detective barked at him.

"It's Mathews. Call a general alarm and get the fire department closest to . . ." he rattled off Carla's address and waited for a confirmation before hanging up and heading for the door. In what seemed to take hours, as if he were swimming through kelp and couldn't make any headway, he managed to reach the kitchen door, but when he grabbed the handle, the metal knob was so hot it instantly burned his hand, and he yowled with pain and fell backwards against the fence that ran along the side path to the backyard. He glanced down at his hand, hot and sore in the palm but almost numb at the fingertips.

But he couldn't think about that now. He had to get into that house. And then he heard the wail of a siren and the wo-oo wo-ooo wo-woo of the police cruisers, and in a matter of seconds all hell broke loose on the street where Carla's house was burning.

Just as Lou Mathews was thinking that the fire trucks had gotten there within seconds and how could that be, two figures

240

came toward him from the backyard, and he saw it was that guy again, Joe, and the woman who was always by his side.

At such a time, when a man of action, like the detective, feels completely at a loss to do something to save the woman he loves, he feels he has to do something, so he lurched at Joe and pulled out his handcuffs, wrenched Joe's arm behind his back, and snapped the cuffs roughly around his wrists. Joe didn't resist. In fact, he was too stunned to make a run for it or try to dematerialize.

Chapter Fifty-One

Moses Freeman's shift began at three in the afternoon. He would not be home when his wife returned from teaching her high-school English class nor see Bobby and Willie when they got home from baseball practice. Hockey was over, and the spring sports were well under way. Soon the games would start, and he'd make every effort to get to as many as possible.

Theoretically, being a captain should have decreased his working hours, but that had not happened. He still went out on some calls with his squad, but he also had a lot of paperwork he never used to have before it was his responsibility to keep the department in top shape. So they practiced and drilled, and he supervised, and everything continued to go smoothly at the fire station. He liked his guys and they liked him.

That night, when the call came to muster—and that happened rarely—no one could say, later, when it was all over, who had taken the call or where it had come from. There had been a call from a police precinct, but by the time that came in, they were already suited up and on the trucks.

With sirens blaring and horns blasting, they made the fifteen-block trip to the house on fire in record time. Geared up and ready to roll, they jumped off the truck and went into action, as prepared as humanly possible, like a dance company performing a well-rehearsed ballet, every step taken with minimum effort, each motion having a distinct function, not one breath wasted, not one finger raised without necessity. They were on the house, up the stairs, inside, water blasting, oxygen tanks in place, boots on, heavy gloves and protective masks and fireproof suits, weighed down in gear, in fact, like soldiers in battlefield conditions.

One of the firemen yelled from the truck, "Hey, that's Carla Patterson's house!"

When Moses heard that, he ran to the front door and hacked his way through as the rest of the squad fanned out, searching for people trapped inside. Flames licked at every surface, and the firemen sprayed noxious retardant as they inched forward. The staircase was badly burned, but Moses yelled to one of his team to back him up, and he took two steps at a time, hugging the wall opposite where the flames burned brightest.

As those manning the truck unleashed streams of water onto the outside of the house, the fireman inside killed it with foam and retardant, while Moses went methodically from room to room, yelling "All clear!" when he found it empty. And then he reached Carla's bedroom. Filled with smoke, it was hard to see inside until he advanced enough to spot a bed and a body under the covers. He didn't stop to see who it was, just scooped her up in his arms, yelling, "Victim needs oxygen!"

She lay limp in his arms as he carried her down the stairs to where the men had put out the flames and smoke now curled up from the charred wood in the fire's aftermath. The squad had fanned out on all three floors, spraying and checking for people and yelling, "All clear!" as they went.

Outside an ambulance packed with on-site equipment was ready with a crew of five to take over for Moses Freeman. He carried the body, who could have been a stranger as far as he was concerned, to the waiting gurney and as gently as possible laid her down. Immediately, a medic placed an oxygen mask over her mouth, and another took her vitals. When he got a strong pulse, he looked up and nodded to Moses that she was alive.

Moses pulled off his mask and unbuckled his oxygen tank, laying it on the ground by his feet, and he came over to look at her for the first time. Her eyes fluttered open. There, standing at her side, looking straight into her eyes, was the son who had only the day before rejected her. Slowly it dawned on him, with the enormity of an avalanche, who he had saved. His throat tightened and he felt faint, wobbled a little, and then an extraordinary thing happened.

Carla reached out her hand and took his and squeezed it. She nodded her head and smiled behind the oxygen. With her other hand she slid it out of her way.

"It's all right, son. You done good tonight. Real good. I'm glad to see you."

Then she closed her eyes and placed the mask back over her mouth, for it had taken all the effort she had left to speak these words.

For Moses, this gentle gesture overwhelmed him, and the tears rolled freely down his face. He knelt down on the cold, hard ground next to the gurney and ever so lightly kissed his mother's cheek. "Mama," he said. "I'm glad you're here."

Then the medics lifted the gurney, one on the front, two on the back, collapsed its legs, and slid it into the back of the truck just as Detective Mathews, flashing his badge, busted his way through the medics and firemen and said, "I'm riding with her." He climbed in before anyone could argue, and off they went to the nearest hospital, with Carla flanked by the two men she loved.

Alanna watched from across the street where she and Joe had gone when Detective Mathews ran off to Carla. It all happened so fast, he forgot to release Joe, who stood next to Alanna, his hands still cuffed in front of him.

"Well, I guess I've got you where I want you now," she joked.

"Shall we find a room so you can have your way with me?"

Before she could answer, one of the firemen walked across the street toward them. At least he was dressed like a fireman, but they soon saw that it was Morgan, having fun all done up in firefighter gear like a kid playing at danger. He grinned at them and raised his hand in a salute.

"Well, you did it, you two. You did just fine. The Committee wants to have a talk with you. But first, I think we'll have to get you out of those restraints. That is, unless you want to go up that way."

Joe held out his hands and Morgan chuckled. He pulled a small key out of a pocket somewhere and clicked the cuffs open.

"You sure have been a thorn in my side, Aloysius Joseph Taft. But I'll miss you." He pulled the cuffs off and pocketed them and the key.

As he rubbed his wrists, Joe flinched at the use of his full name but still caught the hint. So did Alanna, but she was afraid to ask if it meant what she thought it might. Joe wasn't so shy.

"Morgan, you have a way of getting under my skin, and I won't miss that, but does this mean we're done? Is it time to make our decision?"

"Joe, you'll never change will you? After all you've been through, still impatient, impetuous Joe."

"That's not quite fair. I waited a helluva long time for one thing. Longer than I've ever waited before." He glanced at Alanna, but she had turned away so he wouldn't see her blush. It didn't occur to her that the dark of night would give her cover.

"Maybe you'll decide to stay with us for a while longer now that you've found your groove. Some do, you know. Being a

245

Wish Granter has certain advantages. I guess you've appreciated that."

Chapter Fifty-Two

On the following Sunday, just four days after the fire, a little before noon, in the middle of the brunch serving, a father, a mother, and two boys arrived at Carla's Home Cooking. They were dressed in church clothes, the boys neat in creased pants and sweaters. The mother wore a wool hat and a rather heavy wool coat, for it had turned chilly again, probably the last blast of cold before March went out like a lamb. The father wore an overcoat and beneath it a suit and tie.

They sat at a table near the rear, but not right next to a window. Raoul noticed them first and sent a waitress to take their order. Carla was in the back, tasting the vegetable soup that she had asked Raoul to prepare. Carla's soups were among their more popular menu items.

The other favorites, year round, were her chocolate desserts. She offered the most variety of chocolate desserts anywhere in Brooklyn, she would tell just about anyone, any time. This Sunday, there were over twenty-two kinds of chocolate desserts on the menu. Each one personally developed by Carla and created under her direct supervision. In one corner stood a glass case over six feet tall with desserts on round shelves endlessly rotating. The boys noticed it before they sat down and nudged each other.

"You boys behave," their mother snapped. They sat down after taking off their coats and letting their father hang them on one of three coat trees along the wall to the side of the door.

In the kitchen, Raoul was talking to Carla, a soup ladle in her left hand poised above a huge pot, her other hand holding the pot's cover like half of a cymbal, as if she were a member of a marching band.

"Someone out there you gonna wanna see," said Raoul.

Carla looked up from the pot of soup, her eyebrows raised.

"Look to me like your boy come home after all," said Raoul in a quiet voice, knowing how hard the past few days had been, what with the fire and everything. When they sat together in the restaurant after closing two nights before, she finally told Raoul and Lou Mathews about her son. At that moment, the detective was seated at the very same table by a window.

Somehow, Carla's hold on the pot cover loosened and it clattered to the floor. Raoul walked over to pick it up.

"You sure?" Carla asked.

"Pretty so," said Raoul and stooped down to retrieve the cover. He took it to one of the stainless steel sinks and began washing it up. "Go on and look for your own self," he said.

Carla put down the ladle carefully and stripped off the apron she had tied around her middle. Slowly, deliberately, she walked to the door, her fingers knotted together in what could have been a prayer. At the door, she looked out, surveying the restaurant, and there they were. Her family.

"They must have just come from church," Carla said to Raoul. A waiter said, "Excuse me." Carla stepped out of his way so he could get past the door. This was a bad place to be standing.

"What should I do?" she asked Raoul.

"Go on out there and talk to the man," said Raoul. He came to stand beside her. "Ain't no reason to stand here."

Carla finally emerged from the kitchen. She walked over to their table. Moses stood up and held out his hand. She took it in what was not a handshake but a welcome.

248

Then he turned to his family and said, "Boys, I want you to meet Mrs. Carla Patterson, your grandmother."

He turned to Carla, still holding her hand, and said, "Since you've lost your home, at least for a while, we'd be happy if you'd come stay with your family. As long as you need."

Outside, looking in the window, Alanna and Joe smiled. Joe took Alanna's hand in his and squeezed it.

"Well done, Alanna," he whispered.

In a little while, as Joe and Alanna watched the scene on the other side of the window as if it were a play performed just for them, Carla came to the table where Lou Mathews was waiting. She happened to look up and spotted Joe and Alanna smiling at her. They were holding hands, Carla noted. Lou Mathews followed her gaze, and as the two couples looked at each other, Joe and Alanna faded from sight, gone back to meet with The Committee to decide their fate.

"Carla," Lou Mathews said in a voice so low only she could hear it. "Who are those people? Or better yet, what are they?"

"It will take some time to explain it," she said. "But let's just say they've given me my life. My true life, the way it was meant to be lived."

Joe and Alanna whirled through time and space, holding hands all the way. Whatever time it took them to reach The Committee, it was enough to decide where they wanted to go and what they wanted to do next.

L B Gschwandtner is the multiple award-winning author of eight books under her own name and two books under her pen name, Bea Alexander. Her novel, *The Other New Girl*, was a USA Best Book Awards winner and received an honorable mention from Reader Views Literary Awards. You can see all her books at lbgschwandtner.com.

Website: Lbgschwandtner.com
Bluesky: @lbgwriter.bsky.social
Facebook: www.facebook.com/LBGschwandtner
& Bea Alexander Author
https://www.facebook.com/profile.php?id=61571339319956

Books* by L B Gschwandtner

The Other New Girl (Teenagers in trouble at a Quaker boarding school)

The Wish Granters series: They'll grant a woman one wish; the rest is up to her.
Shelly's Second Chance (The Wish Granters, Book One)
Carla's Secret (The Wish Granters, Book Two)
Emma's New Love (The Wish Granters, Book Three – Coming Soon)

The Naked Gardener (a woman gardens naked then goes on a wild canoe trip with gal pals)

Page Truly and The Journey To Nearandfar (a fantasy for middle graders who love adventure and imagining what might be)

Maybelle's Revenge (short stories with a twist)

Foxy's Tale (mother/daughter angst with an incompetent vampire)
Coauthored with Karen Cantwell

Books* by Bea Alexander (pen name)

Recipe For A Witch (YA witchy story about what happens when 18-year-old Amanda discovers she has spellcasting powers)

Escape To Zendara (dystopian love story with multiple plot twists set against the backdrop of a corrupt city)

*Available at Amazon.com or order from your local bookseller.